FIRST LOVE FAREWELL

BOOKS BY ANNE EMERY

Tradition
Bright Horizons
Mountain Laurel
Senior Year
Going Steady
Sorority Girl
Scarlet Royal
Vagabond Summer
County Fair
High Note, Low Note
Campus Melody
Hickory Hill
First Love, True Love
Sweet Sixteen
First Orchid for Pat
Married on Wednesday
A Dream to Touch
First Love Farewell

FIRST LOVE FAREWELL

BY

Anne Emery

PHILADELPHIA

THE WESTMINSTER PRESS

PRINTED IN THE UNITED STATES OF AMERICA

To Mary,
who knows how this story finally ended

THE BIG GYMNASIUM, filled with nine hundred graduates and a couple of thousand parents and friends, was hot. Programs fanned gently or briskly, fathers mopped streaming faces, and the graduates, wearing blue academic gowns, sat patiently through the long, hot ceremony, waiting for release.

Pat Marlowe thought, fanning herself, that it was tragic the way she seemed to be in a state of suspended emotion during this big moment of her life. Graduation from high school was the most important thing that had happened to her so far. Except Tim Davis, of course. She squinted her eyes and searched the thousands of upturned faces of happy parents, trying to discover her own, who would have Tim sitting with them. But the faces merged and swam before her eyes, and she returned to her thoughts while the chorus sang an anthem.

She should be feeling something dramatic during this ceremony, something should be happening to her at this climax which she had frequently believed would never arrive. She stirred stickily inside of the blue gown, mopped her forehead, and looked down the line of graduates near her. They all looked hot. Some were dreamy, some were enduring the ceremony with fortitude, all were patient.

After today she would never be a high school girl again. But instead of triumph, she felt cut adrift. The college world, for all she had looked forward to it, was new and untried. It would be an older world, and in some ways she wasn't ready for the growing pains of getting to the far end of that long road. If she could just get married this summer, she thought, the way she and Tim had once planned, they would be there, at the end of the road, part of the adult world, ready to begin living. And this ordeal of study, preparation, struggling through school, could be bypassed.

This was not rational, she knew perfectly well, and already Tim and she had decided that this summer would be too soon. But it was fun to dream. And this day that closed the door on her high school life recalled all the excitement, the rewards, the unforgettable things that had happened to her in high school. There was Tim, with whom she had fallen in love in her junior year. And the theater, which she had discovered in her senior year, while he was a freshman, away at Crandall College. She smiled at her thoughts, and then, afraid someone might be noticing her, she looked again at the graduates around her. The speaker was talking dramatically, but it sounded like things she had heard before. The third boy in her row was yawning. One of the girls (her name was Barbara, and Pat knew her only slightly) looked very white, and Pat watched her with fascination, wondering what would happen if someone fainted in the middle of the program. But Barbara leaned forward and kept her head down for a few minutes, and when Pat glanced her way again she was sitting up, relieved and excited at having almost caused some confusion.

The speaker was concluding, the chorus rose to their feet, and the graduating class prepared to walk up to the principal and receive their diplomas. The orchestra began the solemn march, and the first line of students rose and went forward. Each name was called, each student paused and faced the audience before he returned to his seat. Pat was in the tenth row, and it would be a long time before her turn came.

Youth was behind her with high school. She would no longer change much. Her mother had talked a great deal about how she and Tim might change in the next year or two. But Pat laughed at that foolish argument. Tim hadn't changed in his freshman year at Crandall. She hadn't changed yet, and she was about to be a freshman. Perhaps when they were married, a year or more from now . . . It was probably a good thing, after all, that they hadn't planned it for this summer. She would have hated to miss the summer theater program at Northwestern University, which she had learned about in the spring. And while Tim did not like the theater, and could not be enthusiastic about her interest, he did agree that she might as well " get it over with " before they got married.

The time had come for her line to move up to the platform, and she stood up, pleased to let her clothes hang away from her body, glad to move after sitting still so long in the heat. She kept her eyes on the boy in front of her: his robe was short and his feet looked awkward, as if he would stumble as he went up the steps to the platform. At that moment he did stumble, and she could see the red coursing up the back of his neck as he recovered his footing.

" Patricia Marlowe," intoned the principal, and she faced

11

the audience and again in that second of time looked for Tim. Then she smiled at the principal, thanked him, and returned to her seat with her former conviction that it was all a dream and she would never remember any of the ceremony, because she could feel nothing. Nothing at all.

And then graduation was over, graduates and parents began to mingle, looking for each other, and the crowd moved through the doors into the hall, where there was a fresh breeze flowing. Her family were waiting for her in the hall, and she moved slowly and patiently with the crowd until she was out of the gymnasium.

She was a graduate, finished with high school, yet still caught in the business of receiving congratulations, of participating in the reception for graduates and parents, of keeping Tim beside her, seeing in his face pride and triumph that she was finally grown up and out of high school.

Her brother Mike — tall, wide-shouldered, bulky beside slender Tim — home from Princeton just in time to see her graduate, threw one arm around her shoulders and exclaimed: "So you made it! Good work, Pat! Where's Connie?"

He looked over her head, discovered Connie Reid across the hall with her own parents, and began to plow through the crowd to reach her.

Twelve-year-old Denny said: "It sure took long enough. Boy, am I thirsty! When can we get something to eat?"

Tim said: "Congratulations, sweetheart. Now I feel as if we're really in step again. It took a long time to get you out of high school."

Mike returned to announce that he was going out to dinner with Connie and the Reids, and Pat's father and

12

mother took her and Denny and Tim to celebrate the triumphant occasion.

Richard Marlowe was president of the chamber of commerce in Allandale, where he had built up the town's most important insurance agency. He was a heavy-set man, inclined to be impatient with youthful chatter, but willing to put up with it on this occasion. He had not approved of Pat's announcement that she was deeply in love with Tim Davis, but after waiting a year to see her discover her mistake, he was resigned, and in fact had become rather fond of Tim. When Pat pressed him to tell her that Tim was nice, he said, "As nice as any of the boys you've had around."

Jo Marlowe wrote stories for magazines, and had gained a national reputation as a writer. She knew that her husband's reaction was only normal: no father thinks the boy his daughter wants to marry is good enough for her. She herself was convinced that this was a situation where parents could only wait patiently. If Tim was truly the love of Pat's life, it would be a mistake to interfere. Optimistically she believed that if Pat was making a mistake, she would find it out for herself. But since Pat and Tim had been talking for a year about getting married someday, she too was resigned to the obvious course of true love.

Denny thought Tim was great, but he could not understand anybody wanting to marry his sister. He had been suppressed on this opinion often enough to have grown discreet between the ages of eleven and twelve, and today he was prepared to dine patiently with his parents and Tim and Pat, because the food would be good and otherwise he would have to go home alone.

13

Tim was tall, with dark eyes and a nice smile. He was attentive to the Marlowes because he liked adults and because he realized that it was important for Pat's parents to like him. He had transferred, at the end of his freshman year, from Crandall College to Northwestern University, because Northwestern offered courses that he could not get at Crandall. So in the fall he and Pat would be going to Northwestern together.

At dinner Tim talked about the job that he would be working at during the summer in his father's hardware store. Pat talked about the summer program at Northwestern University, three miles away in Evanston, where she would be part of the summer theater group. Tim thought he might look around for a new car. Hortense, his present transportation, was very old and beginning to give him trouble. Denny wanted to buy Hortense from him for ten dollars, which he had saved.

Mr. Marlowe said little, letting the young people chatter on. At nine thirty he consulted his watch, said it was time to be getting home, and signaled the waitress to bring the check, with some evidence of relief that the day was over.

Tim thanked him appreciatively for the dinner, they all drove back to Allandale together, and at last Tim and Pat could be alone. They climbed into Hortense and went out to ride along the lake shore.

"How does it feel?" he asked, teasing from the eminence of being a year ahead.

"It feels wonderful to think of being through high school. And yet I hate to leave it behind."

She hesitated to put into words, "That was where we fell in love," hoping Tim would say it for her, would remember without being told.

He smiled nostalgically. " I liked going back — seeing the graduation. I keep remembering when we met in the halls between classes — "

She leaned over and kissed him. He had remembered, and she was blissfully happy.

" But now that we're going to be on campus together, we can do it again."

" But not for three months." He looked vexed. " I don't see why you want that summer program when you could get a job and be making some money."

" But Mother thought I ought to take a chance like this when I can. It might be my last chance for a long time at summer theater work."

He could not argue with her mother's decision.

" But someday you're going to have to learn how to work," he said.

In spite of her part-time jobs during holiday seasons, she had saved nothing, and she had never worked at a full-time summer job. Tim had said frequently before now that she didn't know the value of a dollar, and had no idea of saving money. And this was all true.

" We can't get married," he brooded, " until we've managed to save a lot more than I've got now."

" I know."

She felt an uneasy sense of conflict. Tim thought she was just having a good time playing around with acting, while he was working every spare moment and saving money for their marriage. She believed that everything she could do with theater work was important background for a career in her chosen field. Her mother encouraged her: she was going into the School of Speech at

15

Northwestern, and every experience in that field was valuable.

Tim smiled, but it was an effort.

"I suppose someday you'll get a job," he agreed. "I can wait if you can. Only right now it looks like a long summer, with you spending every day in Evanston until the first of August."

She laughed reassuringly. "I'll be around more than you think," she promised. "I'll be home evenings, and you're going to be working all day anyway. Before we know it summer will be past and we'll both be on campus every day together."

He took her in his arms and some of the uneasy tension between them dissolved.

"All I know," he said with his lips against her hair, "is that everything seems to take so long. And this stage business takes you so far away from me. Let's plan to get married a year from August for sure."

"Tim," she gasped, pulling back to look at him. "Can we? Will we have enough money? Oh, I'll save like mad! Do you really think we could make it that soon?"

He kissed her again, long and hard, and said grandly: "Why not? I've got a good job, forty hours a week all summer, and twenty the rest of the year. I'll have a thousand saved by next year, with thirty to forty-five a week coming in even while I'm in school. Honey, we can do anything we really want to, and together nothing can stop us. I'll be twenty-one, you'll be nineteen —"

It was the nicest graduation gift of all.

2

ON MONDAY, JUNE 17, Pat drove the Marlowes' second car, an old Ford, down to Northwestern University to begin the summer theater program she had looked forward to. As she drove the three miles from Allandale to the campus, she enjoyed the freedom of having her own transportation, half wishing that Tim were driving her, half glad that no one would be waiting to hurry her when she wanted to linger at school to talk to the professor or some of the students.

The summer theater group numbered seventy-five young people, including several from Allandale with whom Pat had worked in high school. She knew within the first hour that Professor Gwynn was going to give her an experience in theater work beyond anything she had found before. He was a spare, energetic, gray-haired man, his hair usually standing up because he buried his hands in it in moments of frenzy, which seemed to occur daily. He was reputed to be the most outstanding director in the university's School of Speech, and Pat, enrapt, felt before the first hour was past that everything she had heard about him had been pallid compared with the personality of the man himself.

The summer theater would present three plays in the

six-week period, with rehearsals until dinnertime daily. The first performances would be given next week. Professor Gwynn handed out scripts, announced auditions for that same afternoon and Tuesday morning. The play would be cast and rehearsals begun by Tuesday afternoon.

On Tuesday she was a few minutes late because of a traffic snarl that held her up for fifteen minutes. She ran across the campus breathless, and came into the theater workshop with high color, pounding heart, and gasping breath that she tried to make unobtrusive. Auditions were already in progress, and she hoped her late entrance would not matter. Professor Gwynn ignored her, except for an accusing stare which did not interrupt the directions he was giving. But Andy Craven, whom she had met in the group yesterday, turned his head deliberately to the back of the room when she entered and smiled a mocking smile as he watched her walk down the center aisle a few steps and sink into the first empty seat. She looked past him at Professor Gwynn, trying to give the impression that she had been there all the time. No one knew the difference, she thought angrily, except that conceited ham who had to turn around and call attention to her.

In spite of herself she had to be interested in Andy's reading: it was obvious at once that he had more than usual talent, and she knew he would get a lead. He was lean and brown, with a rather prominent nose, a teasing glint in his gray eyes, a sensitive mouth that curved wickedly or mockingly most of the time — a gifted actor who took nothing seriously but his acting. He was a graduate of Glendale High School about twenty miles from Allandale, and for the first day Pat had disliked him violently. He seemed to her self-centered, egotistical, conceited; she

18

had told herself driving home on Monday evening that he was all the hard names she could think of, and she couldn't stand him.

But by two o'clock on Tuesday, when she went outside to sit under a tree and learn a few lines before being called back at three to run through the play, she found Andy Craven sitting on the grass leaning against a stone monument. He glanced up as she came out of the door and beckoned her to him with an authoritative gesture.

"Yes, *sir*," she said scathingly. "What can I do for you?"

IIe grinned at her persuasively, and she thought without warning: He's got beautiful eyes. You'd think he was sincere. Then she rejected the thought. She didn't care to have any favorable reactions about Andy, who was too conceited for his own good already.

"I thought you might be willing to work on lines with me," he said. "We've got a couple of scenes together, so we could cue each other, and then I'll cue you on your other lines if you'll do the same for me."

She was about to make a flip retort about preferring to work alone, but some latent good sense deterred her — she knew perfectly well that this was a golden opportunity, that she could learn much more quickly working with someone, and that Andy, whether she disliked him or not, was the kind of person who could give her insight and theatrical knowledge of the job she had to do. Even plain, drudging memory work could add up to more than learning the lines, when you studied with a person of the talent he had indicated in his audition.

"You've got a lot more lines than I have," she objected, wondering why she said it. "However — "

"Penny pincher," he remarked. "If you're going to count out your pennies, I can count too: I'll settle for a line-for-line exchange. Would that be satisfactory? "

She felt a hot flush of embarrassment creep over her up to her hairline, and she looked away, hoping that she could undo the impression she had made. She laughed, deliberately gay and unconsciously excited, louder then she meant to.

"I don't really pinch pennies," she said, looking at Andy and more concerned now with his impression of her than her own of him. "Let's get started and see how far we can get. Your part is the important one, anyway," she threw in generously.

He waved that off, as if he were used to important parts, and said: "Never think the other parts are unimportant. Your lines are just as important as mine are."

She stared at her script for a long time, wishing she could settle down inside. Andy's words jolted her into a reversal of emotion that made her feel as if her mind was churning around trying to find its balance. She admired his gift, and she knew, disliking to believe it, that he took that gift at its face value, as something that required more work than lesser talents, that what she had believed to be conceit was only a mixture of confidence and drive and a sense of humor that derided not only everyone he knew but himself as well. Then she shrugged, slipped into a more comfortable position, and said, "Shall we read it through first? "

She read through her part casually, thinking only about remembering the lines as quickly as possible. But Andy was putting almost as much expression into his reading as if he were already in front of an audience, and before the

20

end of the scene Pat was impelled to match his effort.

"That's strenuous," she said, dropping the script at the conclusion of the scene. "My goodness, do you always memorize like this, as if you were performing?"

He grinned, half deprecating himself. "It takes me so long to decide exactly how I'm going to say each thing, I usually try it a dozen ways before I settle down to an interpretation. So I figure I might as well start practicing on that at the same time I'm doing lines. Sometimes it works."

"Are you going into the School of Speech in college?"

He scowled slightly. "Not next year. I'm going to Mead University, and they haven't got much of a speech department. Although they do put on plays."

"Mead!" Pat was enthralled by the coincidence. "That's where my best friend is going — Connie Reid."

He was not interested in Connie. "Only reason I'm going there," he said, pulling a clover blossom with a long stem and nibbling at it, "is my folks don't want me to go to speech school. They think it's a hard life, and they want me to go into law or engineering or some other 'dependable' profession. Anyway, they say, if I just get a good liberal arts education, I'll know better what I want to do."

Pat contemplated him thoughtfully. "I'm going into School of Speech right here at Northwestern," she said. "But I can always teach, if Broadway or TV or Hollywood are too un-co-operative."

He nodded. "If you can teach, that's fine. But I want to direct and produce, and they think that's too tough to break into." He flung the clover blossom away, and his brown, lean face was hard. "Dad was one of the directors that never quite made the grade," he said. "He just never made any money in the business, and Mom doesn't want me to have all the trouble he had. But I can't see anything else. I'll go to Mead next year and maybe even graduate from there. But someday I'm going to be a director."

"You'd be good," Pat said, feeling objectively critical.

"Of course I'd be good," he said impatiently. "I know what I can do." He glared at her. "It isn't conceit when you *know*," he said flatly as if she had spoken. "I don't overestimate myself. I know what I have to learn and how hard I have to work. But I know where I can go too. Only a stupid person would think that was conceit."

"Well, thanks for calling me stupid," she cried. "If that's the way you're going to be, you can learn your lines alone!"

She jumped to her feet, but he reached out and caught her wrist in a hard grip and pulled her down again.

"Don't be ridiculous," he said authoritatively. "You know it's good for you to work with me. Look at the way your reading technique picked up just going through that one scene. Now, come on. Time's awasting, and we've got a lot to do. Begin again on page fourteen."

Subdued, she went through it again, trying to ignore the impressions that struggled in her mind for recognition. He was bossy — or would you call it masterful? There was a ring of maturity that made him seem older than Tim in some ways, and yet she knew he was younger. And she could not call him conceited any longer. That was not the word. Although she could not define his personality, she had to admire him even while he angered her.

When he said critically at the close of the reading: "That wasn't as good as the first time. What's the matter? Are you afraid of me?" she knew he understood her better than she knew herself.

22

"Good heavens, no," she disclaimed, knowing that she really was a little — afraid of his professional judgment, afraid of his recognizing the weaknesses that she was too scatterbrained or too careless to correct.

"Well, then, pay attention to what you're doing. Good heavens, girl! You can be a lead in one of these plays before the summer is over, if you work. Don't you even care?"

"Certainly I care!" she cried. "What do you think?"

He grinned at her again, that spontaneous, disarming grin that surprised her every time, because it seemed to read her inner meaning, to recognize and laugh at her secret thoughts.

"I think you're lazy," he said.

She flushed. "Maybe," she acceded. "I don't like to work as hard as I should, I know."

"I don't usually like lazy people," he said. Then grinning again, "But sometimes I do."

Tɪᴍ ᴄᴏᴍᴘʟᴀɪɴᴇᴅ bitterly about Pat's never being able to go to the beach with him. He had arranged his working hours from eight to four, so he could have the late afternoon for swimming. She was on campus until dinnertime daily, even on Saturdays. But they were together in the evening, and some days were hot enough to go swimming after dinner. At the end of the first ten days Pat knew, trying not to believe it, that they were running out of things to do and to talk about, as they had last spring vacation when they had been together too much.

She thought about it seriously as she drove down to the campus on Thursday in the last week of June. Final rehearsals were scheduled for the first play, and already they were casting the second with students who were not in the first one, while those who played in the first would work on stage crews for the second. Pat looked forward to the dress rehearsal of her own play, the weekend performances, and the new play all at once. It made her feel taut and wound up, as if she were running in high gear. . . . Would she and Tim run out of things to talk about after they were married? . . . She looked forward to meeting Andy at rehearsal. At least it would be someone to talk to besides Tim — and then, dismayed at such an idea, she tried to stop thinking altogether. But she could not help wishing that she could talk with him as she talked daily with Andy.

The campus was beautiful in June. The lake glittered in the early sun, deep blue today, with small white ruffles. She slowed her steps, gazing at it appreciatively. Catalpa trees dropped fragrant white thimbles in her path, and she drew a deep breath of the summer breeze off the lake, the fresh-cut grass, the sun-warmed pines, the sweet, climbing honeysuckle on the trellis of the Botanical Garden. She was glad to be alive, glad to be here on this ideal summer campus, glad to be doing something different from working in Allandale.

Andy looked up as she arrived at the wings of the stage, where Mr. Gwynn was yelling at one of the girls who had forgotten to bring a wheelchair she had offered. Holding his head in his hands, he moaned: " I don't know why I get into these things! Anybody that directs plays ought to have his head examined. If I live long enough to get through this summer I'll surprise myself. *Who* can find a wheelchair inside of ten minutes? "

" I could probably get one," Andy muttered to Pat. " You come with me." Aloud he said: " I think I can find one, Mr. Gwynn. Give me half an hour. And if Pat will drive the car for me to save parking time, I can get it more quickly."

" It's men like you that keep the theater alive," said Mr. Gwynn. " Andy, if you fail me, this play goes in the lake instead of on the stage."

" ' Old Never-fail ' is what they call me," said Andy. He grabbed Pat's hand and said: " Run, kid. We've got to make time," and he pulled her across the grass at top speed.

"Why didn't Pearl bring that wheelchair?" Pat demanded. "She said it would be so easy, she said she'd put it in the back of her station wagon. Did she just forget it?"

"I don't know," Andy said. "But you can't blame Gwynn for getting mad. She didn't let him know until this morning, and dress rehearsal is this afternoon. Now the first stop is the university infirmary. I'm practically certain they won't have one, but we'll ask. Next stop is a telephone book. There must be a drugstore that supplies things like that for rent."

"Who pays for this?"

"I'll pay for now, and maybe I can get my money back. It shouldn't cost very much to rent a wheelchair for a week, if I pick it up and deliver it myself."

Half an hour later he was pushing Pat in the wheelchair from the parking lot up to the theater and receiving Mr. Gwynn's congratulations on his ingenuity.

"Nothing to it." Andy dusted off his hands, dismissing the matter. "Any other little thing you need? In the meantime I paid out five dollars for yonder rolling chair, and payday isn't till next Wednesday."

"Here." Mr. Gwynn handed him the five dollars. "Now we're half an hour late starting rehearsal because of this nonsense." He made a trumpet of his hands and hallooed at the players sitting around on the grass. "On stage, everybody. Make it snappy or we won't be through in time for lunch."

He was edgy with the strain of final rehearsals — Pat could recognize it. Every director grew tense and irritable the last day before performance. And everyone in the cast unfailingly did his worst, forgetting lines, forgetting business, becoming wooden and stilted. At twelve o'clock Mr. Gwynn hurled his script to the ground and buried his head in his hands again.

"It's terrible," he moaned. "The worst thing I've ever been connected with. O.K., drop it. Forget it. Go get something to eat and be back here at two. Sharp. We'll go through it twice this afternoon. And dress rehearsal tomorrow morning. Get out of my sight, all of you. I've got to be alone!"

Andy took Pat's arm and drew her out of the back door with no loss of time.

"Why don't I run down to the Grill and pick up a couple of sandwiches and some hot coffee to carry out, and we can sit on the beach and eat?"

"It would be lovely," she said. "Here, I'll pay for my own lunch."

"Good girl. Just for that I'll get you a surprise. You wait here, and I'll be back with our meals in ten minutes."

She watched him run down to the gate and across the street, laughing at him. He was fun, he was impetuous and impulsive. And she could not help making comparisons with Tim, who was neither impetuous nor impulsive. Tim wouldn't like to eat on the beach, even though it was a balmy summer day. Or would he today? But she was sure he would never suggest it. Tim liked to do things in an expected manner, in a way planned well in advance. He disliked more than almost anything an unexpected change of plan, an impulsive thought. He liked to be sure what he was doing, to have considered ahead of time what any line of action would lead to, to be sure he was going to enjoy what he was doing. He did not like to take chances. A

27

stable quality, Pat reminded herself. But sometimes the element of chance was fun.

Andy was returning, and she watched him, thinking that she had never noticed before that he was only about three inches taller than she was. Tim stood six feet tall, and she had always admired his height. Never before had height seemed unimportant and she felt as if she were growing up to take that attitude about it.

They went down to the beach and located a sandy spot where the roots of a huge willow were partially uncovered by the water. The day had turned hot and the shade was refreshing.

" Let's wade," said Andy. He leaned down to untie his shoes and grinned up at her. " Ever since I was a little boy I haven't been able to stay out of water. It used to make my mother so mad she couldn't stand it when I'd come home soaking wet every day it rained and made big puddles. But I still like it."

He rolled his slacks up to his knees and rubbed his feet in the sand, watching it pack into damp rolls and heaps. Pat took off her shoes and socks, and the sand was cold and fresh. They sauntered down to the edge of the water and walked through the water along the beach to the next pier, where they climbed out to sit on warm, sunny planks and dangle their feet while they talked.

Pat told Andy about her best friend, Connie Reid, who was working this summer waiting table in Allandale's busiest restaurant.

" She's been going with my older brother, Mike," she said. " She worshiped him for absolutely years, and he never knew she was alive. And then they discovered each other at the end of Mike's senior year." She sighed, remembering those happy days. "However," she became practical again, "when Mike was at college last year they had some kind of misunderstanding, I guess. Anyway, he didn't write enough, and she went out with other boys."

"Why not?" Andy demanded. "How could any girl be silly enough to sit home while her boy was having fun? For all she knew, he'd never come back, and there she'd be, the best years of her life wasted."

"Of course, that's what Tim and I did when he was at Crandall last year."

"Now, how about Tim?" Andy wanted to know. "How serious is this business with him? I mean, are you going steady? engaged? married? Where do I stand in all this?"

She laughed. "We're very serious," she said. "But our parents aren't entirely sure yet that we know what we want." That sounded unconvincing, when she considered it, and she amended it. "I mean, my mother can't seem to feel sure I've met enough men to know that Tim is the one I want. I keep telling her I don't have to meet other men to know, but she thinks — oh, well, you know how parents are. Anyway, Tim and I have agreed to date other people occasionally, just to keep our parents happy. But we hope to get married a year from August when I'm through my freshman year."

Andy was regarding her curiously.

"You mean you're really going to marry this boy? I'd better meet him sometime."

"Oh, you'll meet him! The only thing wrong is that he doesn't like the theater. Sometimes I wonder if I ought to concentrate on it so much next year in college."

"Definitely," Andy assured her. "You'd make a terrible mistake to give up something that means so much to you

29

just because your boy friend doesn't happen to feel the same way about it. In fact, you ought to get another boy friend. Me, for instance."

She laughed again. "Tell me about your girl friends," she challenged him.

He told her about the girl who had broken his heart just before his high school graduation — he was going to be very careful before he let himself in for heartbreak again. He told her about his family, his little brother Jim, who was the same age as Pat's brother Dennis, about his hopes for a career in theater, which his family hoped he would forget.

His family's attitude about his chosen career was very much like her own family's attitude about Tim, Pat thought. Parents never thought you knew what you wanted, never believed you could possibly choose the right thing. She felt that she and Andy had more in common than their theater interest.

"Why don't we go to see that movie at the Crown next week?" he asked. "Did you ever eat at that Italian restaurant over on Simpson Street? You haven't? You haven't lived! I'll take you out to dinner there and we can go to the movie afterward."

She shook her head. "I don't think I can do it," she said. "Tim counts on me every evening, and he feels neglected anyway, with my being away all day."

"I ought to meet my rival someday," Andy said. "This is sparring in the dark when I don't even know what the guy is like."

"I'll set up a beach party," Pat suggested. "You could meet Connie that way. I want you to know her before you both go to Mead. How about Saturday? Oh, I forgot about the play. How about a week from Saturday?"

"Fine. Maybe I can get your boy friend worried."

"Oh, he knows he can count on me."

"Is that good?"

"Isn't it? I mean, if you're planning to marry a girl, shouldn't you be able to count on her?"

He shrugged. "Oh, sure. But next year is a long time away. And all this business of dating other people just to make sure — how do you know something isn't going to come untied?"

She laughed at him, thrusting back a small, cold wave of concern, and they went back to the afternoon rehearsal, refreshed and content with the day, the play, and each other.

~

The performances went off extremely well. Even Mr. Gwynn was astounded and happy. Pat's parents brought Tim to the Saturday night program, and when they met her at intermission they told her they were amazed that her work was so good, this play was far beyond anything she had accomplished before, and they were delighted that she had the opportunity to work with this group.

Tim agreed with everything, but Pat, sensitive to his every thought, knew that his expressions of praise and enthusiasm were only polite, not from the heart. He recognized the quality of her performance and he was glad for her. But he could not enjoy the play, try as he might, and his pleasure came only from his desire to please her, not because he himself was interested. Abruptly the gulf opened again.

"You met Andy Craven tonight," Pat reminded him,

when they were alone. "How did you like him?"

"Oh, he's all right. Why?"

"We had a lot of fun doing this play, and Andy is going to Mead in the fall. I thought it would be fun to have a beach party next Saturday and get him and Connie together."

"O.K., if it doesn't rain. I can't seem to get excited about picnics."

"At least it would be something to do besides going to a movie."

"You're right at that," he said cheerfully. "O.K., honey. You name it, we'll do it."

"You *must* be missing me daytimes," she said jestingly. "You're being so accommodating."

He held her close to him. "I am missing you," he muttered. "It seems as if the summer will never be over."

She kissed him in a long, clinging embrace, and a wave of longing swept over her.

"I almost wish I didn't have to be so far away every day, all day," she murmured.

"Almost?"

"I mean —" she leaned her head on his shoulder and shut her eyes, trying to think clearly, "I wish you were there with me."

"Oh." He sounded disappointed, and she knew just what he was thinking: he would have been happier if she had indicated discontent with her summer, instead of only wishing that he were doing it with her.

They both sat in dark silence, and she wondered in a strange detachment whether this summer of separation that seemed deeper than the separation of his being away at school was going to prove anything for both of them.

32

Ever since they had fallen in love, almost two years ago, her mother had remarked from time to time how little they had in common, and Pat had always laughed off her reflection with the easy assurance that when they got married they would have all they needed in common, in their home and children.

The veil of the future lifted for a moment, and she felt as if she could see clearly her life ten years hence. She would be cleaning the house, children would be scrambling on the floor, Tim would be coming home for dinner. She would say: "There's a wonderful play on TV tonight. I've been looking forward to it all day." What would he say? "You go ahead and look at it, honey. You know I don't like TV —"

She closed her eyes and shook her head to clear her thoughts. She loved Tim just as he was, she told herself. She had loved him so long, she was so used to him. She knew what he was like, and she didn't care. It was impossible to imagine living without him.

She turned toward him in sudden urgency.

"Kiss me, darling. I love you so much, Tim!"

His kiss seemed to dissolve the dark shadows that threatened her security.

THE WEATHER on Saturday night was perfect — hot and clear, with the water a clean, deep blue. The sun was just sinking as they carried the food from the car to the beach and collected wood for the fire.

Connie and Andy got along fine, teasing, scolding, chasing and splashing each other, while Pat knew, deep-down, that he was only having fun with Connie. He had brought a ukulele and he kept plinking notes that sounded questioning, astounded, hungry, happy. Tim laughed more than Pat had ever seen him, and Connie wiped tears of mirth from her eyes.

They raced together to the raft, and Tim was the first one there, the first one off the diving board. Later Andy challenged him to a race to the life line, and again Tim won. Pat was bursting with pride, and Tim glowed with satisfaction as he came out of the water, his lean, tall frame muscular and strong. Andy followed him, smaller, slighter, grinning happily as he threw himself on the sand. A crowd was more fun than a twosome, and Tim was enjoying himself.

"We ought to do things like this more often," Pat murmured, as Andy and Connie went off to find more wood for the fire. "I mean, go out with a crowd. How do you like Andy?"

"He's O.K., I guess. He seems to get along with Connie all right. You're not trying to fix anything up between them, are you?"

She laughed and shook her head. "There isn't going to be any romance there. I can tell. Connie is still fond of Mike."

"Funny kind of fondness when she dates the way she does."

"Aren't we supposed to be dating others too?" She cocked an eyebrow teasingly.

"For us, it's different. We know what we're doing — just passing the time till next summer."

She watched a stream of sand trickle from her closed hand in the firelight, content. Without letting the thought light for more than a moment, she knew that diluting Tim's company with Andy's lighthearted camaraderie was healthy, that she liked Tim all the more because of the change.

"How do you really like Andy?" she asked again, when the evening had ended and they were alone.

"He's all right. Not my type."

"We have so much fun on campus in these plays we're doing. He's great in the theater, really great. Did I tell you we hated each other the first day?"

"Anybody that wouldn't like you at first sight must be a dope."

"No, just temperamental. But interesting."

Tim said nothing. When they stopped in front of Pat's house he turned toward her.

"I can hardly wait for school to start this fall. You seem

35

so remote this summer. It worries me."

"You don't need to worry," she told him softly.

~

Every day now was paced with fast-driving rehearsal for the last play that would be given — too soon, it seemed. Each performance amazed Pat with the polish Mr. Gwynn had communicated to his summer actors. And while Pat was not performing this time, she was working on stage and make-up crews, and glad to have a reason to stay through every rehearsal. Time was so short; she hated to think that this engrossing experience would end so soon.

She would be a freshman in the School of Speech on this same campus in the fall, she reminded herself. But it would never be quite the same as this first bright discovery, and she sighed to see this happy time go by. Sometimes, she thought, looking into the years ahead, the future was more uncertain than it had ever been.

Once she said to her mother, "I just don't know, Mother. With the way Tim feels about the theater, I don't know how this is going to work out."

She was lying on her bed after dinner, waiting for Tim to come over, staring at the ceiling and thinking as she waited. Her mother looked up from clean laundry she was sorting into piles on Pat's chaise, and then, alert to the distress in her daughter's voice, she came over and sat down on the end of her bed.

"I think your problem is basic, Pat. You felt this way once before, didn't you? I'd think it out very carefully, test your ideas, go very, very slowly."

"But we've been going together so long," Pat wailed.

36

"I don't know what I'd do without him. I can't *imagine* life without Tim!"

She thought over and over again of the conversation she had had with Joanne Miner, Connie's sister, whom she had talked to when this same frightening realization had struck her last spring. Joanne was living with her parents while she waited for Jerry to return from Naval duty. Her baby was now three months old, plump and charming, and Pat remembered him longingly. If you had a baby, perhaps nothing else mattered. Joanne had said she and Jerry liked different things. But unfortunately there were so few things that Pat and Tim really liked together: bridge and bowling and dancing. Could you build a lifetime of recreation around bridge and bowling? Neither she nor Tim cared enough about dancing to invent new steps or practice rhumbas at home.

She wondered suddenly how Andy liked dancing. He had mentioned square dancing, and she loved that. But Tim didn't know how, nor did he care to learn. Restlessly she turned her thoughts away from the unsatisfactory subject, and she heard Tim's step on the porch with relief.

In the last week of play rehearsal and production she was not able to see much of Tim: rehearsals went into the evenings until nine thirty, ten, ten thirty, and in rebellion at ending something she loved so much, she joined the rest of the cast for coffee and pizza after rehearsal every night.

There was so much to talk about: Andy wanted to travel; he wanted to get a job in New York next summer, so he could see the shows; the year after that he wanted to work in professional summer theater.

"We never did get to that Italian restaurant," he said

37

regretfully. "Maybe I'll take you there during some vacation, if you can ever get a night off."

"When you come home from Mead, I'll go out with you," she promised.

"How about after summer session?"

She thought about that a moment before she answered.

"I'd love to see you, Andy. Maybe we could double some night."

"Maybe. But that wasn't what I had in mind."

He lighted a match and watched it burn, his eyes dark and moody. Pat waited, watching his eyes, the outline of his brows, the thin face that could quicken so vividly into gaiety. She thought of all the fun they'd had together, and how comfortable were these silences with Andy. He looked up seriously.

"Mind if I say something?"

"Please do."

"Well — I don't think Tim is the right man for you, Pat. It isn't because I'm jealous or anything. I don't even know if I'd step in if he did step out. I'm not being romantic, and I don't know if we'd ever be that way. But we've had a lot of fun together and I like you too much to see you get hurt. I mean, I just don't think Tim is the right one. And I'd hate to see you make a mistake. I think too much of you."

"Well, thank you for thinking of me," she said, oddly disappointed that he disclaimed romance. "But you don't know Tim the way I do. We're very much in love."

Andy grinned at her suddenly, as if he thought that she did not know her own mind.

"Let me know if you ever break up."

"You're the first one I'll tell."

38

He kissed her good night and good-by, and she thought if she ever did break up with Tim, she could get interested in Andy — very easily.

~

Now that summer theater had ended, Pat found herself looking forward impatiently to the opening of school again. She planned clothes for her college wardrobe, she met Connie between working hours and went window-shopping, comparing styles, prices, choices. Tim scoffed at the whole idea. "You've got more clothes than you need already," he decreed. "It's a waste of money to keep buying things you don't need." But she ignored him and enjoyed the shopping. Clothes were so delightful!

Mail began coming for her from the university, and her calendar was full of notes and dates: freshman week, rush week, clothes needed (sweaters and skirts for this party, simple wool dress for another, dressy afternoon clothes, heels, blazer, formal for an evening party).

Tim came over to have lunch with her every day at twelve, sometimes at her house, sometimes at a sandwich shop next to the hardware store. He had rearranged his working hours, so that he worked from ten to three daytimes, and from six to nine in the evenings. At three thirty every sunny day he picked Pat up to go to the beach for a couple of hours. He had missed her during those weeks when she was in Evanston every day, and he wanted to spend as much time together as possible to make up for it.

It had been a year, Pat recalled, since she and Tim had been together every single day for hours at a time. And it was such a pleasant habit to have her day planned around him, to drive with him while he made deliveries, to return home at nine thirty in the evening and plan their future in nightly talks.

"The customers think they never saw a place like Davis' for service," he told Pat happily. "Not many stores these days deliver in the evenings. I took a load of peat moss over to Mr. Finnegan the other night about seven, and he was tickled to death. He said: 'I was just saying if I had that peat I'd do a little work in the garden nice night like this, and five minutes later you drive up with it. Have I got Aladdin's lamp or something?' I said, 'Davis is just as good as Aladdin any day,' and he roared."

He talked about how they could improve the service even more, different lines he thought they should carry, ideas for window displays, advertising that would bring customers flocking to the door. He talked as if he owned the shop himself.

"But I thought you didn't want to work in the hardware store when you finished college," Pat said, surprised at his new interest in his father's business.

"Not immediately after college. I'd like a little experience in other places. But someday Dad is going to want me to take over, and it's a nice little business."

She listened, trying to be as much interested as Tim was, because someday the hardware store would be an important part of her life. She wondered if she would do the work his mother was now doing, and if she would enjoy it. Inventory in a hardware store, bookkeeping, waiting on customers was a far cry from the theater. She wondered how they would fit together, whether there would be time for both.

"You know, Dad is paying me a dollar and a half an hour," Tim told her. "We can get married a year from

40

now, the way things are going. I'll have that thousand in savings, I'll have another thousand for tuition for junior and senior years, and about thirty dollars a week coming in. And then in the summers we could get a little more ahead."

" I could work at least ten hours a week," Pat said, fired with anticipation. " Baron's or Sinclair's could use me evenings and Saturdays — "

Even as she offered to work, the thought shot across her mind that she might not be able to take part in any plays if she tied up her time so that she could not attend rehearsals, and a chilly feeling of doubt stiffened her for a moment.

" A year from now," Tim said. " We'll set the date in the spring, and perhaps your folks will announce the engagement then."

Next August. A year from now she would be getting married. Strange that she did not feel more excitement about the idea. But she told herself that a year was a long time. She would be really excited in the spring when the announcement could be published. They would have to find an apartment, but of course not till a few weeks before the wedding. . . . She was disturbed that the whole project seemed unreal, like talking about a dream.

" Mom thinks it's a great idea," Tim went on. " She's crazy about you, too."

" Oh, I like your mother so much. I can't wait till next year."

Down underneath she knew she could wait very easily. The coming college year, like this summer's work, was too good to miss.

41

CHAPTER

5

AFTER THE FIRST WEEK Pat was used to being away from
the campus, and summer theater had become a pleasant
dream, so that sometimes she wondered if she had really
spent those first six weeks in such high delight. Life in
Allandale with Tim seemed so normal now.

A card from Andy told her that he was leaving next
week for New England, before he went to school in the
fall, and he was stopping in New York for a week to see
some shows. Lucky, lucky, lucky, Pat thought, feeling
that she was hearing from another world. Then she picked
up a letter with a Wisconsin postmark, and gasped with
excitement.

Tim's Aunt Lucy Cooper, who lived on a farm near
Madison, hoped that Pat could come up with Tim the last
week of August and spend a week with them. Tim had
talked so much about the farm that Pat felt as if she already knew and loved Aunt Lucy and Uncle Harry and
the life they lived. The idea of going up with Tim was too
delightful to happen to her; she could not believe her
parents would let her go: her father would think she saw
too much of Tim already; her mother would have other
plans. She did not let herself count on anything, and astonishingly, her father said he thought a week on a farm

might be a nice vacation for her.

She had hardly recovered from the shock of this decision, at the dinner table, when Tim called, almost too excited to talk, at seven o'clock.

"Pat? I just bought a yellow convertible."

"You *what?*"

"I got a new car. A yellow convertible, white sidewalls, radio. 1951. It's a dreamboat." He was almost incoherent with delight.

"But, Tim, how did this happen?"

"You know my friend Rocky, in the gas station down the street from the store, where we have all our work done? Well, he had a customer who wanted to sell this car, and he called me about it. About an hour ago. So I went over and got it."

"Tim, I've got to see it."

"I'll be there in fifteen minutes. We'll take it out on deliveries tonight."

She hung up the telephone and sat down, dazed and incredulous. Not only a car, but a yellow convertible — an impulsive, dashing gesture that seemed so adventurous that it was unlike Tim. But it was a bright omen that he could thus, on an impulse, spend hard-earned money for a car that represented to him drama, romance, sheer unnecessary pleasure!

Tim drove up to the house and came in swaggering with triumph, bubbling with boyish delight. Pat loved him in that mood: he seemed so vulnerable and yet so successful that she could enter into his mood fully and be as much excited as he was.

They drove around for two hours, making deliveries, trying out the car, which did indeed seem to be in good condition, responsive, all the satisfactory things Tim said it was. They put the top up and down, bought some foolish caps to hold their hair in the wind, waved to their friends, and celebrated joyously.

"We'll drive up to the farm in this," Tim said. " Pretty nice, isn't she? I'm going to call her Eloise."

Pretty nice, indeed. But by the end of the evening the glow had faded, and in spite of her pleasure Pat was tired of talking about the car.

"I've got a lot to do before we go up to the farm," she remarked. " The notice for new students came in the mail today. I've got to sign up for rushing by the end of the week."

"You aren't going through rushing, are you? "

"Why, certainly I am. Why not? "

He turned into her street and stopped in front of her house. "Do you really want to join a sorority? " he demanded.

" I won't know until I meet the girls, but I think it would be fun. I think it would be a good idea if you pledged a fraternity."

" Not me! I'm a confirmed independent. I don't approve of fraternities, and I'm not going to have anything to do with them."

She was eager to discuss the question which she had been turning over in her mind all summer.

" But fraternities and sororities are nothing like the high school business you disapproved of," she said. " In college they're more civilized. Anyway, I think it would be fun. And at Northwestern they're important."

He shook his head, and a cloud settled over his face, a cloud of disagreement.

44

" I never heard anything about sororities or fraternities that I liked, and I don't expect to," he said flatly. " I think they're snobbish and undemocratic and expensive. I wish you wouldn't pledge, honey. The girls will want you to go out with fraternity boys. They probably wouldn't want you to go with me — "

" That's the most ridiculous thing I ever heard of! I wouldn't belong to a group that felt that way. I just want to go through rush and meet the girls and see what I think of them. I'm not going to close the door without even seeing what's on the other side."

" Let's go into the house," he said, sounding tired. " I'd like to talk to your mother."

They went in silently, both thinking about this new disagreement which had come up between them so unexpectedly at the moment they seemed closest together, and found Mrs. Marlowe sitting on the screened porch reading a magazine.

She looked up as Pat and Tim came out on the porch.

" Hi, kids. Want to find yourselves a cold drink? "

" Later." Pat sank down. " Unless you want us to fix one for you."

" I'm not in any hurry," said her mother. " Have you got something on your minds? "

" How did you know? " Her mother's intuition never failed to astonish Pat.

" I could feel it."

" I guess it really isn't important," Tim said. He spoke slowly, studying his hands as he did so, as if he were trying to figure out just how important it really was. Then he looked up at Mrs. Marlowe. " Do you want Pat to be a sorority girl, Mrs. Marlowe? How do you feel about it? "

Mrs. Marlowe closed her magazine and looked from one to the other.

"I'm neutral," she said. "There are arguments on both sides. When I say I'm neutral, I mean I'm not going to push Pat into something or keep her out of something necessarily. She'll have to decide for herself. But it might be a good thing, Tim. You know how Pat likes people. She's the kind of girl who ought to belong to an organization. Since she'll be living off campus, a sorority house would give her a place where she'd feel at home. But if she doesn't find a group she wants to belong to, or if she isn't invited — that isn't too important, either. She can have a good life at college without belonging. The whole thing depends on her meeting the girls and deciding how she feels about them and how they feel about her. But I see nothing wrong with belonging to a sorority when Greek organizations are as important as they are on this campus."

Tim said no more, but he looked discontented. To him, Pat knew, college was simply a study routine to get through, with as little diversion as possible, meanwhile working and saving money to get married. He would be interested in nothing that would not lead to that goal.

But for her, college looked like a world of excitement and fulfillment and fun. The classes were a necessary discipline which she would accept in order to enjoy the plays, the dances, the football games, the new friends she was going to make. And this delightful world of people and color and politics and parties was something she would not want to cut short. She did not look forward to intellectual stimulation in any field but the theater. She was not academically inclined. But both her parents and Pat

46

herself felt that the varied life of a university campus would be better experience than the concentrated professional dramatic school.

Already the fun was beginning, in getting ready: receiving the correspondence for new students, planning and shopping for still more new clothes, the thought of seeing Mr. Gwynn again and some of the students with whom she had worked this summer. It could all be so much more fun if Tim would enter into it with her, take the same interest in his college future as she did in hers, look forward to rush parties.

There was another long silence. The telephone rang sharply, and Pat went to answer it.

"Tim," she said over her shoulder, "do you want to get some lemonade or Coke while I'm on the phone?"

He got up as if he were relieved that the discussion of sororities was at an end for the time being, and went to the kitchen for the cold drinks, while she picked up the telephone in the living room.

"Why, Andy!" she cried. "How wonderful to hear from you! . . . Yes, I got your card. When are you leaving? . . . Oh, I wish I could see you before you leave! . . . " Tim went back to the porch with a tray of glasses, glancing at her as he passed with a gesture that meant "Hurry up!" She turned her back on him and spoke into the telephone again. "I'd love to have you come out here some day before you leave for college. You can tell me about those New York shows! Oh, Andy, have a wonderful, wonderful time. And thanks for calling."

She hung up the telephone, swept with nostalgia for the early summer. For a moment she was back again on campus, walking with Andy, and he was saying, "Wasn't that

47

a great moment when — " and " I got a chill right down my spine — " It had been a great moment, the chill had gone down her spine too, and Pat remembered it clearly: one of the big thrills of the summer. She buried her face in her hands and sat very still, wishing she could live it over again, wishing she could see Andy right now, struggling with a nostalgia that was so acute she could feel it like a pain. She lifted her head and sat back, looking at the telephone again, and thinking quietly for a long time. Then she went back to Tim on the porch.

" So I had a chance to buy this car, a 1951 convertible, for a hundred bucks! " Tim was saying to her father, with the gleeful air of one who has made a million-dollar coup in the stock market. " I always wanted a convertible, and here it is. And is it a car, man! "

Pat had heard the whole story twice already; he had told it to her in detail while they were driving around. She smiled at him because she loved his boyish pride, and thought about something else while he went on and on about the steal he had in his new car: white sidewalls, only ten thousand miles on them, new battery, new transmission twenty thousand miles back, new top, overdrive, " The works. And only a hundred bucks! I'm selling Hortense for forty-five dollars, so this dreamboat only cost me fifty-five dollars — "

She loved the car too, but she was tired of talking about the car with the name commensurate with its bright, sophisticated air: Eloise. She thought again of Andy's call, and Andy's conversation, and the sparkling facets of Andy's company, and she wondered why she felt like crying.

IT HAD SEEMED incredible enough when her parents had agreed to let her spend this week with Tim's aunt and uncle. It had seemed impossible that they should let her drive up with him.

There had been pessimistic conversations about highway travel, how well Eloise would take the trip, reminders of Mike's accident last Christmas when one of his schoolmates was killed.

Surprisingly, Mr. Marlowe was the one who refused to be fatalistic.

"Tim's a good driver," he conceded. "I don't see why we should anticipate trouble. It's only a couple of hundred miles, isn't it, Tim? And you're leaving before the traffic gets heavy in the morning?"

Pat was still surprised to find herself on the road at six o'clock in the morning on a bright day in late August. But here she was, the surprise was beginning to wear off, and she felt that this trip must be a confirmation of her parents' acceptance of their love. Even her father was no longer resisting the idea that she was one day going to marry Tim.

"Next year we'll be going off like this on our honeymoon," she murmured. Tim reached over and gripped her hands firmly with one of his, steering easily and surely with the other.

"I hate to think of waiting a year," he said.

"Even one more year won't seem so long when we're together at college," she said. He was silent for a moment.

"If you're going to pledge a sorority, I feel as if I'll never see you on campus."

"Oh, honey, there's no connection in that argument. Nobody is going to come between us."

He shrugged, pessimistic in a sudden swing of mood.

"You don't know what it's like. I saw it at Crandall. They have different standards, and sororities and fraternities stand together on them."

"They can't push me around. I wouldn't stand for it."

"Then why join?"

"But, Tim, I'd like to be part of a group of girls, eat dinner with them sometimes, go to the house for lunch. I like things like home-coming floats and parades. I can still do all the things you like: we can study together and meet for coffee. And I'm counting on going to the football games with you."

"That's one thing you don't have to worry about," he said with a half grin. "I'm not keen about crowds, and I don't like football well enough to sit out in that stadium every Saturday afternoon."

"You aren't going to the football games! Oh, honestly, Tim, how can you be like that? How can you go to college and not even care whether your football team is playing or not?"

"Oh, it isn't hard! I'm going to college to get a degree, and all these juvenile distractions leave me cold. I'm not going to waste my time doing anything I don't want to do."

"Well, then, I'll go with the sorority girls, because I'm going to every single game. I wouldn't miss a single one of them."

"If you insist on being a sorority girl, there are a million good reasons for joining."

"If you insist on not wanting to do anything at college except study, that's one more reason for me to join a group to have fun with."

They followed a curving, black-topped road, winding through woods that were densely green and fragrant with the scent of summer, in a silence that was chilly with disagreement.

Tim leaned back and drove easily, watching the road, his mouth straight and hard. Pat looked out of the open window on her side, noticing the white birch trees clumped among thick trunks of oak and maple, chestnut, and occasional pine. Already the summer green was overcast with gold, and leaves dropped lightly and lazily, now one by one, now a handful drifting through the still air. Summer was coming to its end, and when this summer was gone there would be only three more seasons until her wedding day. Perhaps they could come up this very road again next year —

"Tim, darling," she turned to him, "we'll have to understand each other as we go through this next year. We can't argue about things like this when we're married."

Eyes on the road, he swung the wheel with an easy motion of his left arm.

"Nope," he agreed. "We ought to like more things together."

51

She was chilled again with a feeling of emergency. This kind of critical difference came upon them thus unexpectedly, always at a time when they seemed to be getting along so well.

What was it that Joanne Miner had said last spring, when Pat had talked to her about the problem?

"If you lean on each other too much, you can wear out your love and come to the point where you want to be alone for a while." And further, "You and he ought to be able to spend some time apart, with other people, when each of you has a special interest."

Pat agreed with all of that. The trouble was that Tim did not feel that way. He wanted to spend every free moment with her, and yet there was not enough common ground to support such a load of companionship.

"We'll like things together when we're married," she began. "We'll want to fix things up — and buy things —" She remembered that they had never been able to decide on either silver or china that they both liked, and she stopped a minute. "Anyway, if we love each other we can solve any problem," she said at last, more confidently than she felt. But she had to say it, because she had to have something she could rely on.

～

The week at the farm seemed to prove something. Tim was happy to be up there: he took so much pride and pleasure in working with his uncle in the fields, with the livestock, tinkering with the machinery, that Pat felt love flowering as if it were new, just to see him thus content in an environment he loved. He took her riding on the tractor across fields, he showed her how he could tote hundred-pound bales of straw, he drove her into town in the jeep for shopping, they rode the horses, which he did very well and could teach her how to do.

The weather was beautiful all week; the air was filled with sun, and the sound of crickets, and arching flights of grasshoppers, and the fragrance of the dried hay. Sun, sounds, scents were all magnified in this quiet countryside, where the days flowed past slowly yet quickly, filled with tasks that must be finished, yet leisurely.

Pat spent much of her time with Tim's aunt, who said to call her Aunt Lucy, as if she were already part of the family, baking bread, helping to prepare dinner for Tim and his uncle and the hired men, running the vacuum cleaner after meals, stacking the dishes in the dishwasher while Aunt Lucy put away food.

She loved Aunt Lucy, who was deeply interested in Tim's romance, and they talked about plans by the hour. She felt, by the end of the week, that Tim's family had accepted her completely, and that she would be perfectly happy belonging to that family. She hated to leave when the week was up, and she agreed fervently with Tim that they would rather live on a farm than anywhere else.

The Tuesday after Labor Day, Tim put her on the train at ten in the morning, and she felt as she had a year ago when he had gone off to Crandall: her sense of loss almost overwhelmed her, the more so because she had grown so fond of the Coopers and the farm. She knew this sadness was foolish, since Tim would be returning within a week, but she wept a little, not trying to restrain her tears, because she knew that Tim was pleased that she cared so much. And for an hour as the train ran toward Chicago she enjoyed a period of melancholy, sure that her love must be deathless for her to feel this heartbroken over a short separation.

After an hour she was feeling more cheerful in spite of herself, and her thoughts turned toward the coming preparations for the school year. Mike would be leaving for Princeton next Friday. Connie would be going to Mead on Sunday. Andy was coming out tomorrow afternoon to say good-by. She began thinking about Andy, but she was not going to let herself look forward too much, because he would be leaving on Sunday too. She was not yet ready for rushing: there was one more dress she had to find.

The feeling of urgency and pressure tightened every nerve and she sat taut, making a mental list of all the things she must do before rushing began. Vacation was over, life had begun to race again, and with one backward glance of appreciative nostalgia for the quiet unhurried week at the farm, she looked forward to the coming year like a racer waiting for the starting gun.

~

Pat left for Evanston on Thursday, September 19, for rush week. She was going to live on campus for this period. This meant that Tim would not see her until the week was over, which was one of his reasons for being aggrieved at her insistence on going through rush, but Pat found it was one of the most satisfying aspects of rushing. Her roommate was Betty Donnell, whom she had known slightly at Allandale High School. Betty was a tall, slender girl with a wide smile, deep dimples, and a positive air about making decisions that Pat found comforting. She had been a high-ranking student in high school, Pat remembered, and she had always been pleasant, although

54

they had not spent enough time together to be close friends.

She and Betty had chosen three of the same parties at the same time, and were delighted to find each other there. It was comforting to go back to the room and have someone to discuss rush problems with.

They found on Monday that neither had been invited back to the houses they had liked on Saturday. Both had been invited to the Alphas, which neither could remember clearly.

"What are you going to do?" Pat demanded. "I'm so worn out and mixed up, I'd just as soon drop out now and figure this out later."

"I'm going to finish rush," Betty announced with decision. "I can't remember the Alphas now, but I'm going to their party and give them a chance. After all, who could remember all the girls, in that rat race last week?"

This made sense, and Pat felt grateful to have the decision taken out of her hands. She went to four parties that day, and at two of them Betty was there too. Late that evening, when the parties were over, Tim called, and Pat talked to him for half an hour.

Over breakfast the next morning, she and Betty discussed the next step.

"Tim is terribly lonesome," Pat said. "He's missing me, while I'm staying on campus. And what with not wanting me to join a sorority anyway, it makes everything twice as difficult."

"Ed is a Delt at Illinois," Betty said. "I know he wants me to be a sorority girl."

She had been going with Ed Metzger, Pat had learned, for a year last June. This was just six months less time than

Pat had been going with Tim, and she felt at once that she and Betty had something very basic in common. Ed was a sophomore at the University of Illinois, writing to Betty steadily and giving her advice he thought a freshmen must need. Betty believed that she was deeply in love with him, and expected him to give her his fraternity pin sometime soon. In the meantime she was hedging the possibility of failure in this direction by dating other boys. The trouble was, there weren't very many other boys, and sometimes Pat thought she looked a little anxious.

"I don't know what Ed would say if I didn't pledge a sorority," she said. "How did you feel about the Alphas?"

"I liked them better than the others. I'm going to their final party, along with a couple of others I didn't like as well. And I just might pledge them. I'm not entirely sure. This last party ought to tell."

Betty's mouth hardened a little.

"I'm definitely going to pledge something. Any group is better than no group, as far as I'm concerned, and I like the Alphas just fine."

"I don't care too much," Pat reflected. "But I think Mother wants me to pledge. I think she thinks it will push me into going out with other boys besides Tim. But I think it would be fun, even if her idea is subversive. Let's go and see what's in today's mail."

Among the invitations there was one from the Alphas for each of them.

"Well, the others are out," Pat said, looking at them. "I guess it'll be the Alphas — if they ask me after this party."

Three days later Pat and Betty pledged Alpha at a luncheon party, with twenty-five other pledges. Looking them over, Pat felt they were all wonderful girls, and she was going to be very happy with her sorority.

She moved out of the dormitory that night to make way for incoming girls who had waited until after rush week to arrive, and drove back home, anxious to show her parents her pledge ribbons, sorry that she must leave the campus housing, wishing she could live there.

Tim came over within an hour of her arrival, as delighted to see her as if they had been separated for a year. She showed him her pledge ribbons, and he inspected them indifferently.

"I hope it isn't going to make any difference."

"But, darling, of course it isn't. You can come to the house — boys do, you know. And the girls can help me with my studies. And I can take you to the sorority parties."

He looked unconvinced but resigned.

"O.K., O.K. Want me to pick you up tomorrow morning? I'm going down for registration, and then I'll be driving to school every day. If you want to go at eight when 1 go, we can ride down together."

"I'd love it! Oh, Tim, it's going to be a wonderful year, going to school with you again! Remember that year in high school?"

Life had been so romantic and uncomplicated then, she thought, wistfully. As they grew older it should be even better. But still, those early days had had a freshness and an excitement about them that had somehow worn off since then.

A NEW WORLD opened up for Pat in college, a world she had not really believed existed: a world of new friends, new activities, new interests, a busy world where she found herself running from class to sorority house, back to the campus, to committee meetings, to class again, to the Grill for coffee several times a day, to the house for dinner several nights a week, to study hall or more meetings.

Saturday was filled with luncheon before the game and a hilarious trek with the girls to the football stadium, where she sat in the cheering section raising a white card to form part of the huge *N* when the cheerleaders directed them. She loved school, she loved Northwestern, she loved everything she was doing and everyone she knew, and she saw Tim daily and nightly. The only cloud on this bright horizon was his attitude.

Tim was a serious student; since he cared for so few other activities, he was absorbed in making a good record in his studies. And he could not understand Pat's casual attitude toward her classes.

"But they're so dull," she protested. "The professor doesn't come half the time. The graduate student that takes the class for him doesn't know how to teach. He marks a theme C or D without a word to explain what is wrong or how to change it. Why should I get excited about a class like that? "

" But you ought to care about getting good grades."

"Oh, I'd like good grades. But don't worry about me. I'm learning lots of things outside of class."

" But you won't even be around very long if you don't study more."

" I'm not going to flunk out," she promised impatiently. "I'm having too much fun to lose out on this. You ought to get something out of college besides grades, Tim. You ought to have more fun."

" It takes all my time to study," he said, looking melancholy. " It's just a good thing I don't like social life and activities. This school is harder than Crandall was last year. You don't realize what you're up against."

He refused to go to football games, after the opening one. He said he had to work, and he spent the weekends in the hardware store. But Pat knew that he preferred to work and was glad of so good an excuse to stay away. Optimistically she thought this might be symbolic of the way they were going to resolve all their conflicts. And the solution was the more satisfactory in that she was having more fun cheering with a crowd of hysterical fans than she would have had sitting alone with Tim.

After each game the sororities held open house, and Pat met fraternity men and visiting students from other schools. She urged Tim to come to the open houses, and the one time he did she presented him proudly to her friends. But after that he said he was too busy to spend every Saturday afternoon fooling around with parties, and he would see her in the evening anyway.

59

The girls all liked him. They assured Pat that he was a doll and she was lucky to have such a nice boy attached to her. They were so attentive to him that once in a while it was almost a nuisance. However, their attentions convinced Tim that all sorority girls were not snobbish about independent men, and his complaints about her affiliation faded out.

He arrived every morning at her house at seven forty to take her to school, joining the family breakfasting in the kitchen, teasing Denny, who was usually sleepy and grumpy at that time of day, praising Mrs. Marlowe's coffee, urging Pat to hurry. He had said, early in the quarter, that he was waiting to get his breakfast at the Grill, since his parents rose an hour later than he did.

"No, thank you," he said to offers of breakfast at first. "Well, another cup of coffee would taste pretty good, but I don't need any toast."

The fourth morning he accepted the toast, saying he did get hungry before he got to Evanston. And after that he joined them for breakfast as if he enjoyed eating with a family.

Mr. Marlowe looked at him over his coffee with a quizzical expression, as if he wondered how long he was going to have company for breakfast. Mrs. Marlowe was cordial the first few weeks. After that she said very little, save: "Good morning, Tim. Do you want to pour yourself a cup of coffee?" To Pat she said, with more than a touch of impatience, one evening, "It does seem as if we have enough going on in the mornings without one more person to feed all the time."

But if Pat was going to ride to Evanston with Tim, and she was going to, determinedly, he had to be there at breakfast time, and if he was there when the family were eating, Mrs. Marlowe felt obliged to feed him too.

Another problem arose which Pat had not anticipated. She was a slow starter in the mornings. When her alarm sounded at seven, it took all the character she could muster to pull herself out of bed. And at that time of day she was hardly awake enough to muster any self-discipline at all. One morning she fell asleep again, unwittingly, after she had shut off the alarm. When Tim arrived, her mother called impatiently: " Pat? What on earth is keeping you? Tim is here and you haven't eaten yet! "

Pat was shocked enough to spring immediately out of bed and call down: " I'll be there in five minutes, Mother. Tell Tim I just got delayed, and give him some coffee, will you, please? "

When she arrived at the table ten minutes later Tim was annoyed but patient. She drank her coffee hastily as she put on her coat and said: " I'll get a roll at the Grill, Mother. I don't want to keep Tim waiting. It's impossible to park if we get there after eight fifteen."

Tim waited as she flew through the house, looking for books, for an important paper, and at the same time trying to make up for her tardiness by unwonted concern and attention. At eight twelve, in irritated silence, he followed her out to the car.

He leaned over the wheel and pushed the starting button on Eloise, not having said a word since she had come downstairs. Pat looked at him. His mouth was a straight, angry line, and she moved closer to him and said coaxingly: " I'm really sorry about this morning, Tim. Don't be mad at me."

" Well, it just seems so stupid to be late," he said grumpily. "I like to be on time. I'm the prompt type. And it makes me madder than anything else to be held up because you're always late."

"But I'm not always late," Pat defended herself. "That's not fair, Tim. This is only the second time this year."

He shrugged. "But who knows how many other times there will be?"

"If you don't want to drive me to school," she said icily, moving to the far side of the seat, "I can drive down by myself."

Two miles later he said, good-humored again: "I don't want to drive down to Evanston without you, Pat. I love picking you up in the mornings. But this parking is enough of a problem to get priority. If I have to choose between you and a parking space, you lose."

She smiled at him, happy again. He was really very even-tempered, and she felt remorsefully that she couldn't blame him for being cross this morning. She resolved never to keep him waiting again. The parking space he regularly occupied was filled, as he had known it would be, and they rode around looking for another for several minutes, finally leaving the car six blocks from the campus.

"For a walk like this we might as well take the public transportation," he grumbled, locking the doors.

"I know." Pat was penitent. "It was all my fault. But it is a pretty day, isn't it?"

It was a bright, beautiful October day. The elms were golden in the fall sunlight and dropping their golden leaves casually and beautifully through the sparkling air. The brilliant rose-red foliage of a winged euonymus

62

flamed against some evergreens near the campus, and Pat caught her breath at its brilliance.

"Oh, Tim, isn't that gorgeous? This is the most beautiful time of the year."

"Yep, it's pretty," he said, giving the rose-red bush only casual notice.

"I hate to go inside." Pat slowed her steps, looking up at the intensely blue sky beyond the golden elm hanging over the sidewalk.

He pulled her along. "After all this delay I want another cup of coffee. Come on, honey, let's not dawdle."

She thought momentarily of telling him to go on ahead, that she would join him later. But, with a last glance at the flaming bush, she decided against staying alone.

For Pat, people were the most important thing in her world. She liked almost everyone, she liked company, she especially liked the company of men and boys, and her greatest problem was how to study when she was alone, because without company it was difficult to concentrate. So now, even to look at the fall colors for another moment, she disliked being alone.

As she entered the Grill with Tim, someone yelled: "Here's Pat and Tim! Hi, kids! We've been saving a place for you."

Two of Pat's sorority sisters were waving over the top of a booth to them. Betty Donnell, who drove down from Allandale in her own car, was sitting with Carol Conrad, who was blond, rather dumpy, and usually skittish and overeager in the presence of any man — even Tim, who was openly Pat's property.

"How's my boy friend?" she cooed, pushing along the seat and making room for Tim to sit down beside her.

Pat gave her a baleful glance — not jealous, because who could be jealous of a nitwit like Carol? — but bored with the act she put on so frantically. Carol acted as if she didn't even see Pat, leaning her cheek on her clasped hands and batting her eyelashes at Tim in a come-hither glance so obvious as to be ridiculous.

But Tim loved it. He grinned at Carol happily and sat down beside her, playing up to her manner with pleasure.

"How's my little dumpling doll?" He reached for her jelly doughnut and ate it. Pat felt very patient about the whole scene. Yesterday he had eaten Carol's sweet roll and Carol had slapped him playfully and tried to snatch it from him, wrestling and fussing until Pat had said coldly: "All right, Carol, you can break it up now. Tim will buy you another one."

Today Carol said only: "I was saving that for you, sweetie-pie. You always look so lean and hungry when you come in in the mornings."

Tim winked at Pat as if he knew she would enjoy a good joke with him, and then patted Carol's hand comfortingly.

"Better I should eat it than you, dumpling."

Carol laughed happily. "Easiest way to cut calories I know — just feed them to you."

Honestly, Pat thought, in an access of weariness with Carol, if she'd known Carol Conrad was going to be a sorority sister of hers, she didn't think she could have faced it. All the other girls were wonderful, she liked them all — well, almost all! But Carol was the edge. A legacy to the chapter her grandmother, her mother, and two aunts had belonged to, she was one of those duds that every sorority or fraternity must accept at one time or another. She was not, Pat resolved at that moment, going to sit with

64

Carol for coffee one more morning. It was impossible. She turned to Betty Donnell and murmured: " Someone ought to speak to her about the way she acts in public. I should think the whole chapter would be humiliated."

" It's embarrassing," Betty agreed, with a disparaging sidelong glance at Carol. " But you don't have to worry as far as Tim's concerned."

" I'm not worried," Pat disclaimed. " Just bored."

Nor did she need to worry. Tim had never been sought after as he was this year on campus, and he was flattered as any man would be. Pat, who loved attention herself, could understand exactly how he felt about having even Carol make a fuss over him. Pat could laugh at him a little, she could let him know that it flattered her, too, to have her man the object of the attentions of other girls. And Tim laughed at it himself, when they left the Grill and walked over to class together.

" If you're going to be running around with fraternity men, I might just take Carol out some night," he teased her.

" You think you could stand her nonsense for a whole date? "

" Oh, it isn't hard to take."

" Honestly, Tim! Sometimes I think you have no discrimination at all."

" Darling, I don't want to date anyone but you. You know that. I'm just telling you, I don't want you dating other people either."

She thought that over. " I'd probably be safer with you dating Carol than anyone else I could think of."

He shuddered. " It's a pretty grim fate. You're safer than you know."

They separated, Pat for freshman English, Tim for business history. They had no classes together at all.

"I won't see you for lunch today," she said. "I have to eat at the house."

He looked forlorn. "I'll just grab a bite at the Grill and study over the noon hour, I guess. But we'll eat together tomorrow?"

"Tomorrow we can drive up home, if you want to."

Three days a week she ate lunch at the sorority house. The other two days, when neither had a class between eleven thirty and one thirty, they drove back to Allandale, where they went to Tim's house one day and to her house the other day for lunch. When Pat had work to do at the School of Speech until late in the day, Tim waited for her, studying at the library until she was ready to leave. When she stayed at the house for chapter dinner and pledge meeting on Monday nights, he came back from Allandale and took her home.

"You don't think the sorority is going to come between us now, do you?" she asked, during a break in an evening study session. "All the girls are crazy about you."

"It's working out better than I thought it would," he conceded. "They're nice girls. Not nearly as snobbish as I thought they would be."

"The fall party is coming up on Saturday, and it sounds like fun," she told him. "It will be an informal party at a barn out in the country with square dancing and bingo games going on."

"Square dancing?" He sounded dismayed, and she suddenly remembered Andy, who loved square dancing.

"It's going to be loads of fun," she said firmly. "Do you want me to get us a double date?"

"We could always go with Carol Conrad," he grinned at her teasingly.

"Not Carol," Pat said firmly. "But we could go with Betty Donnell, maybe. Her Ed is coming from Illinois for the party."

"She's a nice kid," Tim agreed. "Why don't you try that? Did she tell you we're in the same math class? "

"No, are you? That's wonderful! She's terrific in math. In fact, she's a brain. Well, I'll see if she wouldn't like to double with us. . . . Did I tell you I have to stay on campus for play rehearsal every night this week? "

"Are you involved in that already? " he grimaced.

"Oh, this is going to be a wonderful play," she told him eagerly. "The girl who's got the lead is one of the most talented actresses I've ever seen. I've only got a bit part, but it's even more fun than it was this summer. You'll have to see it, Tim — you'll love it."

"Maybe," he said, noncommittally. "But are you going to have to hang around until all hours this week? How are you going to get home so late at night? "

"I thought maybe you'd like to pick me up," she said, raising her eyes demurely and opening them wide. "You'd be coming over to study if we were home, and this way we can be together. Do you mind? "

"I don't mind taking you home, but I get kind of bored sitting around waiting to do it," he said frankly.

"Couldn't you study at Scott until this is over? " She tried to plan something that would make the waiting pleasant. "We'll be through at nine thirty, and then I could join you there for coffee before we go home."

"O.K. I probably wouldn't get a chance to see you otherwise."

"Probably not. I appreciate this a great deal, Tim. But it's more important to have a chance to see you than anything else."

He kissed her, holding her close.

"Sometimes I wonder how everything is going to come out," he muttered. "So many things seem to be happening, so many other people and activities. All I want is for us to be together without all these distractions."

But the distractions were so fascinating, Pat thought as she watched him leave.

8

THE NIGHT of the barn dance turned out to be a special celebration: the team had won its third victory of the season. Pat rode back to Allandale with Betty Donnell and Ed Metzger after the festive open house, feeling like an extra wheel, wishing Tim had been there, wishing he shared those hysterical moments when her world seemed to spin and glow with an iridescent flame compounded of youth and romance and hilarity. She knew her parents never felt that flame, and she thought, wistful for the swift flight of time, This is what they mean when they keep talking about Youth. She felt sorry for everyone, including herself, who could not be young forever, and she thought with heart-dropping unease of Tim, who sometimes hardly seemed young any more.

She jumped out of the car at her house and said, "See you kids tonight, then," slamming the door shut. "It was nice to meet you, Ed. We should have fun at the barn."

Ed leaned forward at the wheel and grinned around Betty. He was shorter than Tim, rather stocky, with a blond flat-top haircut, blue eyes gleaming with satirical humor, and a wide face with sloping planes and blunt nose and chin, very different from Tim's dark, narrow, long face and angular height. Though not as nice as Tim, Pat thought with automatic loyalty, he did seem to be nice, and she was delighted that he and Betty were doubling with Tim and herself tonight.

When Tim picked her up at eight they went at once to Betty's house, where they could spend an hour before going on to the dance. Ed was already there, and he opened the door for them. Pat introduced Tim, and the boys shook hands cordially. Pat unbuttoned her coat, and as she began to take it off, Ed lifted it deftly from her shoulders and laid it on a chair.

"Thank you," she smiled up at him. "I'm not used to this kind of attention."

"We'll have to get you used to it." He laid his hands on her shoulders, and as she looked up, he winked down at her.

Pat smiled again, moving away from his hands and smiling back over her shoulder as she took Tim's arm to go into Betty's living room. It was such fun to flirt with all the boys, and have it mean nothing. It was a gay, light-hearted satisfaction to feel so attractive, to persuade oneself that one was irresistible, to have a good-looking boy, any boy at all, corroborate that idea.

"You boys go on in and get acquainted," she said, smiling from one to the other. "I'll go on up and see if I can help Betty. I want to talk to her anyway."

She found Betty in her bedroom, undecided between two dresses, and Pat sat down on a little rocker, pleased to have a minute alone with Betty.

"Ed is darling," she said. "I know Tim is going to like him."

Betty shook herself into a full-skirted dress made in a
70

squaw style, and Pat jumped up to help her find the zipper in the middle of the back.

"I wish he were taller," Betty said. "I always have to wear flats when I'm out with him." She hunted through her dresser drawers and hung a chain of silver beads around her neck and heavy silver bracelets on one wrist. "You know, I'm crazy about that boy, and he says he's crazy about me. He ought to give me his fraternity pin any minute. I thought just maybe this weekend — " she looked pensive. "Until he does I'm not going to let him feel too sure. That's the easiest way to lose a man."

When could you let a man feel sure of you, safely? Pat wondered. She felt sure of Tim, and she had never wanted to keep him uncertain about her feelings. But Tim was different. They had been going together two years this coming Christmas, and surely in that length of time you knew what you wanted. Even their jesting threats about dating other people were based entirely on the idea of co-operating with parents' foolish ideas, not on any thought of discovering another love.

Pat thought of last year, when Tim had been away at Crandall — she had worried about another girl and dated another boy, and it had been a miserable year. And now, after that year apart, they were more firmly attached than ever. They were going to be married next August, she reminded herself with a small quiver, although they had not talked about it since school had begun.

"Anyway, I'm glad we're going together," she repeated. "We ought to double-date more often, Betty. It's so much more fun that way."

Then she wished she had not said that quite so strongly. The trouble was, it was true. She and Tim had found it difficult to fill their Saturday evenings since school had begun, unless there was a school affair to go to. Tim disliked movies, although more often than not, that was where they went. He disliked concerts; he was not interested in plays in Chicago, and besides, they cost too much. Pat suggested a roller-skating evening, and Tim said he hadn't been on skates since he was twelve, and didn't want to learn over again.

The disloyal thought crossed her mind that Tim didn't really like to do anything, and she repressed it. She loved him anyway, and that was all that counted. But a date with another couple would be twice as much fun as spending the evening with Tim alone, even at the barn dance.

"Shall we go down?" Betty suggested. "I've got a new record I want you to hear before we go. We've got plenty of time."

They listened to the record, reviewed the afternoon excitement, Ed talked about parties he had gone to at Illinois, while Betty watched him broodingly, and then it was time to go.

Although half an hour earlier Pat had recognized the pleasure of flirting with someone new and had even thought it was nice that Tim found the same fun with the girls in the Grill, now, when he picked up Betty's coat and held it for her, Pat found herself watching them with sudden irritation.

"Hi, doll," Tim said, smiling over Betty's shoulder as she turned her face toward him.

"Why, thank you, sir. How nice to have someone hold my coat at the right height."

"We kind of match, don't we?"

Betty flashed a bright smile at him.

72

"I could even wear heels with you, I'll bet."

"Come on." Ed was holding Pat's coat. "Let's get the show on the road."

She no longer felt like flirting, but she made an effort to control her annoyance. Why was Tim so quick to grab someone else's coat? she wondered. She had half a dozen angry remarks on the tip of her tongue, and she bit her lip to keep from saying anything. Never let him know you care about it, she kept telling herself.

They climbed into the car, Betty and Ed in the back seat, Pat beside Tim up in front, and she watched out of the window steadfastly until her anger subsided. By the time they had reached the barn, where the party was being held, she could almost laugh at herself. But she took care to hand her coat to Tim and let him check it for her.

"You keep the checks," she said casually. "You'll be getting it for me, anyway."

The first square dance was forming, and Betty and Ed joined the nearest square, which needed one more couple.

"There's no place for us in this one," Tim said, sounding pleased. "Let's sit over here and watch."

Pat was sure she could have found a square, but she did not argue, and they watched the dance from the side line. She tapped her foot to the rhythm, wishing she were out there on the floor. Andy would have loved it, she thought.

The next dance was a bop number, and Tim was proud of his bop. He danced energetically, pulling and twisting Pat about in time to the music, with an expression of working intensely hard. When they sat down again, Betty and Ed joined them.

"Let's trade this one," Tim suggested.

Pat had planned all along to trade dances with different

couples. Whereas most girls disliked trading dances, she knew the boys enjoyed it, and she was frank to admit that Tim was not an extremely versatile or smooth dancer. She would have enjoyed dancing with several of the other boys there. But it was disconcerting to have the suggestion come from him.

However, Ed turned out to be deft and smooth, and she liked dancing with him, especially to the waltz music. When the dance was ended they went back to their table and watched for Tim and Betty to join them. The music began again; after a pause, and the dance again was bop.

"Do you like this stuff?" Ed asked Pat, one eyebrow cocked up.

She shrugged. "It's all right, but I like smooth dancing better."

"Let's sit it out. Where do you suppose Tim and Betty went?"

"Perhaps they went out to the fountain for a cold drink."

"I'll go get us something," Ed offered. "Sure you don't mind waiting alone for a minute?"

"Not at all."

He returned after a short while with frosty glasses in his hand, and they sat in companionable silence, Pat's eyes on the dance floor. Without surprise she saw Tim dancing with Betty again.

"How about that?" Ed commented. "They were supposed to join us after the last dance."

Pat said nothing, watching them as they stayed in a small area of the floor. Tim was eagerly engrossed in the dance, and at the end he supported Betty with his arm around her waist as she bent over backward almost to the floor. Pat's eyes narrowed, and she wondered uncom-

74

fortably if she was not a good enough dancer herself to be an interesting partner. And then as Tim's dancing became more and more enthusiastic and he looked more and more gratified with himself, she became very uneasy.

Leaning her elbows on the table, she said to Ed, "Tell me, Ed, what do you think of the way they're dancing?"

"Too strenuous for me. Why? Do you like it?"

"I hate it," Pat said forcibly. "But Tim and Betty look awfully pleased with themselves."

"Better Tim should do it than me," Ed said lazily. "You know, you're pretty smooth yourself when the music is right. Save me another dance before we go home."

"How come you haven't given Betty a pin?" Pat asked.

He grinned at her mischievously. "Don't you know that's one of those questions you just don't ask?"

"I ask," she said frankly. "I'm interested in these things. You're going steady, aren't you?"

Ed's eyes, too, were fixed on the gyrating couple on the dance floor.

"Just one of those things," he said indifferently. "Neither one of us wants to spend the year sitting home without dates, me down there, her up here. I'll probably pin her by the end of the year."

The sooner the better, Pat thought intensely. She had never seen Tim dance like that with another girl before, and his evident pleasure made her deeply uneasy. Was it just any other girl, she wondered, or was he getting interested in Betty Donnell?

They left the dance floor then and returned to Ed and Pat, Betty leading Tim by the hand, smiling brilliantly upon the two waiting for them. Tim faked exhaustion and sank down in a chair next to Pat.

"Tim is a marvelous bop artist," Betty exclaimed. Funny, Pat thought, she had never noticed before how loud Betty's voice was. "He's really great! Did you see some of those steps?"

"I saw them," Pat said, trying to keep her voice normal. "I always told him he was good. Didn't I, darling?"

Tim smiled happily. "Something about Betty brings out the artist in me, I guess. But it's strenuous work."

He was too tired to dance the next number, he told Pat, and they sat through it together, watching Betty and Ed join another square dance.

Tim had enjoyed dancing with Betty Donnell too much for comfort, Pat thought, too much for the lighthearted flirtation she had been enjoying earlier this same evening. It wasn't possible for him to get interested in someone else, not after all this time, not after two years of being in love! The idea buzzed around in her mind like an annoying fly, and she tried to ignore it.

After the dance they dropped Betty and Ed off at Betty's house and drove on to Pat's. They sat in the car for a few minutes to discuss implications and memories of the dance.

"Betty must certainly be crazy about Ed," Tim observed, and Pat was pleased that he had said it first.

Pat nodded, her head comfortably against Tim's shoulder. "Betty says they're going to get married as soon as they can plan how to support themselves. He's working his way through school, you know, the way you are, but he hasn't got anything in the bank yet." And then something popped out which she had had no intention of saying at all. "Wouldn't it be fun to have a double wedding next August, if they could plan to get married by then?"

Even as she heard herself saying the words she cried,

76

silently: NO, NO, NO! I don't want to share my wedding with anyone.

"Oh, I don't know," Tim said reassuringly. "It's too far away to make any plans, but I don't know that I'd care about a double wedding."

She was relieved to know he felt that way, in spite of her own suggestion, so relieved that she did not even notice, until much later that night, that he spoke of the wedding as " too far away to make plans."

WITH FEWER CLASSES and more time between them than she had had in high school, Pat had the illusion that college was easy. This was a comfortable illusion, and she did not try to dispute it. There were so many delightful things to do besides study. Ten thirty was the coffee hour, when almost everyone she knew met at the Grill. Tim was always there, a dozen of her sorority sisters, including Betty, students from the School of Speech, members of the cast of the current play: Pat knew them all, and through her Tim knew them all.

Her mother said once, " I don't see how you can afford to lose an hour out of every morning at the Grill." But Pat, secure in her illusion, insisted that since "everyone on campus" took that hour out in the morning, she could take it too.

The last week in October was Homecoming, with the freshmen responsible for the Alpha float. Pat devoted most of her spare time for the entire week to the float, including Thursday evening and all of Friday before the parade. Tim worked with her, and drove the truck, at Pat's behest. He enjoyed the effort: all the girls let him and Pat know they thought he was delightful and accommodating. And

Betty said: "I don't know what we'd do without a man, Pat. You seem to be the only one who can get one for us."

That was true. The other girls were dating fraternity men who had to work on their own floats, or else, as upperclassmen, disliked the work and refused to get involved.

When the weekend was over, the game won, the returning alumni feted at open-house teas after the game, and the celebration parties attended, Pat realized that she had not opened a book for four days, and a term paper was due for her English professor on Monday. She sat down Sunday afternoon to work.

But her mind kept springing away from "Fitzgerald as a symbol of his era" to think about Tim. Questions kept intruding, and the safe haven of marriage next summer was a beacon light that attracted her imagination as a flame attracts a moth — the idea that after next summer she would never again have to worry about holding Tim.

She sat and stared into space, dreaming for ten minutes at a time, and then drove herself back to her typewriter to compose another paragraph for her professor, who had indicated on earlier papers that he thought she was not working hard enough. But she had been uneasy about the way Tim had danced with Betty; she made a mental note not to trade dances with Betty again, not ever. And then she told herself not to be ridiculous, there was nothing to worry about. But, again, after next summer . . . She let herself go in a new flight of dreams.

When Tim arrived that evening, the paper was half complete in first draft, and, complaining about her lamentable study habits, he sat down happily to edit and compose and see that she finished the assignment.

Although Tim was in none of her classes, he was interested in the freshman English, because he had had it himself last year, and he knew the kind of themes they wanted. When she was studying geology he had a flair for scanning a paragraph and asking her a question that tested her information. The help he gave her and the satisfaction he found in doing this definite and constructive work made their study sessions some of the happiest times they spent together, although Pat frequently grew tired of the prolonged concentration and found herself wishing they could do other things with the same degree of pleasure.

The quarter was flying past. Mid-terms came the week after Homecoming, and Pat failed two. Now she was beset by a sense of urgency about studying which she had managed to ignore before. She had to study more, she kept telling herself. And Tim, who scolded her about the exams she had failed, came over every night in the week to study with her.

She knew that he disapproved of her casual attitude about her studies, but at the same time he felt superior in this field, and even while she appeared flighty and juvenile, Tim was pleased to help her to improve her mind. Studying with Tim gave a special satisfaction to her work beyond any inner response to the challenge of freshman English or geology. And Tim enjoyed working more than playing: when he was completing a difficult assignment of his own, or drilling Pat on geological questions until he was sure she knew the material, he felt that he was accomplishing something worth-while, which was the highest praise he could give any activity.

Pat tried to persuade him that drama was worth-while, that creative effort in the theater and artistic performances

80

gave the world something important. But these values escaped him completely — either he was entertained and felt that he was wasting his time if he allowed himself to be entertained too often, or else he was uneasy in the presence of artistic power and took refuge in boredom.

After a weekend of dates for which they could find nothing to do that satisfied both of them, Pat thought of bridge.

"We haven't played for ages," she said. "We could get another couple, and it would be fun."

Bridge was a recreation that Tim liked. He enjoyed using his mind, and the mathematical aspects of contract appealed to him. He brightened at once.

"Maybe I could get Betty Donnell," Pat said. "But what man can we get?"

"There's a guy in one of my classes that I've been studying with," Tim said. "Joe Simpson. I don't think he's going with anyone, and he'd make a good foursome with Betty."

"We'll ask them to my house next Saturday," Pat said. "How about Betty? Could Joe pick her up?"

Tim shook his head. "Joe hasn't got a car. But I could pick up both of them and bring them here."

"Fine," said Pat, not thinking about it. She wanted to get some amusing tallies she had seen, they would want something to eat and drink — already her thoughts ranged ahead to a planned party.

Tim arrived with Betty and Joe at eight on Saturday night, and Pat threw open the door. "Hi, kids! I'm so glad you could come. Joe, I'm delighted to meet you."

Joe Simpson was as tall as Tim, brown-haired, gray-eyed, with a friendly smile, an air of being immediately at home. He handled the cards as if he was an expert, shuffling and fanning them out on the table so they could draw for partners.

"I guess you and I are going to take on Tim and Betty," Joe said to Pat, as they faced four cards up on the table.

"Fine!" Pat forced herself to smile brilliantly. "Lucky for me, anyway. Do you feel lucky tonight?"

He seated her at the bridge table and went around to take the chair facing her. It was strange to be playing against Tim, Pat thought, watching him deal the cards. She had assumed that of course she would be his partner. But what difference did it make?

Betty fanned out her cards in her hand and smiled knowingly at Tim. She had deep dimples when she smiled, and Tim was grinning at her as if they had a secret understanding.

"I'll bid a heart," he said.

"Two clubs," said Joe.

"Two diamonds," cried Betty.

"Three clubs," said Pat.

The bid went around again, as Tim raised Betty's diamonds and she raised his hearts, after which he complimented her on being a good girl, and assured her that they had the game in the bag.

Pat felt a vicious satisfaction in setting them three tricks.

While Joe dealt the next hand Betty leaned forward across the table and said to Tim, "Did you get that calculus problem on page 85?"

"I worked an hour on that one," Tim said. "I had a lot of trouble with it. What answer did you get?"

Betty smiled, at once triumphant and mischievous, and

told him her answer. He shook his head.

"I got that one first, but I know it wasn't right. I got this other answer after another hour's work. You'd better let me show you how to do it."

"I should show you," she declared.

They wrangled cozily for another moment, and then Pat picked up her hand and said: "Get on with the bridge game, you two. What do you bid, Joe?"

This time Betty took the bid and played the hand with quick sureness, making two tricks over her bid. Pat felt slow and stupid as she watched her, and Tim congratulated his partner warmly.

He likes a good bridge player, Pat thought, feeling numb. I'll have to get a lot of practice.

The jests and quips about the math class, the students in it, the professor, the assignments, the controversial answers, the mid-term grades went on and on.

"I'm getting tired of math," Pat announced at eleven o'clock, as they threw down the cards and prepared to have some food. "Joe, do you think it's socially correct to talk all night long about your love affair with a math book, when nobody else really cares?"

She was beginning to be angry, and if her tone was sharp, she didn't care. Joe laughed, smoothing out the tension.

"It isn't correct to talk about math," he agreed. "But I can think of nothing more delightful than for you to tell me all about your love affair with the theater."

"Oh, are you interested in the theater?"

"Mad about it. I used to be in all my high school plays, and then I went into the Army and we had talent shows and things to entertain the men, and then when I got out — " He followed her into the kitchen and helped her carry iced drinks and potato chips and sandwiches back to the living room.

Pat was enthralled. Not since Andy had left for Mead had she been able to talk like this. Tim and Betty settled down at the bridge table again, working out problems on the back of a sheet of score paper, and Pat beckoned Joe toward another corner where two chairs were grouped together. They talked about television, actors and actresses, movie stars, Broadway hits, the shows they had seen, the shows they had missed —

" Say, aren't you two going to play any more bridge? "

Tim's question broke into their conversation, and Pat glanced up as if she had been far, far away.

" Are you through with that fascinating math problem? " she demanded. " I thought we'd have a couple more rubbers. We're changing partners, aren't we? "

For the rest of the evening she played with Tim, who ended the evening with the high score.

" Want to ride along while I take Joe back to Evanston? " Tim asked, including both girls in the question.

" Certainly," Pat said. As she and Betty put on their coats she asked Betty, " What do you hear from Ed these days? "

" Oh, he's having a wonderful time," Betty said, shrugging into her coat. " He's practically too busy to write. I hear about once a week. He's dating other girls, but so far it's a lot of different ones."

" Do you think you can get his pin? "

" Well — " Betty was not going to commit herself on that question. " We've both agreed that we can't just sit home all these years, waiting for vacations. Why, I'd miss half

84

the fun of college if I couldn't ever get to a dance. And he can't come up very often — "

Pat followed her out to Tim's car, thinking she'd feel better if Betty were wearing Ed's pin.

"I don't think I'd want to be pinned until I was ready to settle down to one man," she said, thinking aloud.

Betty laughed, a gay, loud, hilarious sound.

"Ed and I understand each other," she averred confidently. "Nobody else means anything at all to me, but just in case anything should ever break us up, I wouldn't want to be permanently out of circulation. Life is too short."

But Betty wasn't having many other dates, Pat knew. She wondered if Betty had the same fearful sense of insecurity she herself felt so often. And, looking at Betty, she knew that Betty did.

Time was so long, so uncertain. Anything could happen when your man was far away like that. She snuggled close to Tim and tucked her hand under his. He squeezed it close with a quick downward glance. Reassurance swept over her in a comforting wave: Tim and she were together, and next August was now only nine months away.

They took Betty home and then dropped Joe Simpson at the Williamses', where he worked for his board and room, and turned back to Allandale.

Alone with Tim, Pat chattered happily about the evening just past.

"Did you have fun?" she asked.

"That was great," he said on a note of surprise. "We ought to do it more often."

"That's what I thought. We could take turns at different houses."

"We could play at my house next Saturday. Joe's a good kid, isn't he?"

"He's delightful. And Betty's fun."

"She's O.K. I didn't like her at first. But when you get used to her, she's all right."

Pat let out a long-held breath, unconsciously. "Remember last spring when we ran out of things to do? We should have had a bridge game going then."

Tim smiled, remembering something about the evening that had pleased him.

"I'll have to ask Betty when I see her on Monday how she made out with that problem we were working on. She wouldn't believe me when I told her it was tricky."

"What was it about?" Pat tried sincerely to understand his interest in mathematical ideas.

"You wouldn't understand," he said, intent on the road which was dark and winding at this point. "It takes a mathematical background —"

She felt shut out again, and withdrew to her own side of the front seat, staring silently at the reflector signs that flashed past them: "Dangerous Curve," "Slow," "Yield the Right of Way," "Caution."

There was something symbolic about all those warnings, but she dared not think what it was.

10

FINAL EXAMINATIONS were coming up the second week in December, and Pat settled down to serious studying. With Tim's interest in her work, she felt that they were on more solid ground as a couple than at any time since high school. His opinion of her work habits was similar to her family's opinion, and he told her frankly that she didn't know how to work.

"We certainly can't get married until you know how to do a job of work better than you do now."

She looked at him, eyes wide, not believing what she heard. She knew her failings, but she could not seem to cope with them. Sometimes she contemplated her weaknesses with a detached consideration, telling herself exactly what she needed to do, and, for two days, doing it. She did not think she was lazy, but she admitted that her efforts were scattered and un-co-ordinated. She said, "I just can't seem to develop good study habits," feeling that this was a reasonable and acceptable explanation for all her troubles. When Tim scoffed at this explanation and told her she was too immature for college, she dropped the whole subject, saying only, "I know exactly what is wrong with me, and I don't care to hear any more about it."

One night in mid-November her mother was sitting in

the living room while she was arguing with Tim, and he looked over at Mrs. Marlowe. Pat glanced at her mother and saw her raise her eyebrows and smile, with a small gesture of her shoulders that indicated, " I agree with you entirely." Pat looked immediately at Tim and saw him shaking his head and drawing down his mouth in a manner that meant, " She's a hopeless case, but I'm still trying."

Infuriated by this exchange of understanding between her mother and Tim, Pat got up abruptly and went to the kitchen to get some coffee for them. She leaned against the sink, arms folded, chin down, battling with her anger. She wanted to throw something, to stamp and yell at Tim that she hated him, to shriek at her mother that she was getting out of this house where everyone kept an eye on her, where everyone knew what she was doing and thought it was wrong.

As quickly as it had boiled up, her anger faded out. She knew they were both right, she knew she was not doing a good job with her studies. Carefully she poured hot coffee into two cups, and called to her mother, " Would you like a cup of coffee? "

" No, thanks."

When she returned to the living room with the coffee cups, her mother had withdrawn to the TV room and she and Tim were alone. Pat picked up her geology notes and began to concentrate with fresh determination. If she had no other motive in life for studying, she did want to please Tim, and someday she wanted to hear him say: " Wonderful work, Pat! I'm proud of you! "

With this incentive, then, she worked doggedly night after night to a degree that she felt was heroic, and that

88

Tim seemed to take for granted as the minimum. She knew she was learning the subject matter, however belatedly, but, more important, this effort she and Tim were making together was creating a new satisfaction in their relationship; she relied on him, she depended on him to help her study, and she knew that he was deeply pleased that she needed him.

When Thanksgiving weekend came he declared time out for the holiday. They would do something just for fun, he said. They could play bridge Friday night, because Betty would be available, and Ed was home for the weekend. He had mentioned it to Betty in math class on Wednesday, and she thought it would be great fun. In fact, Tim thought it would be a brilliant idea to have a tournament game, running from Wednesday night through Saturday.

Pat recoiled a little inside from such an intensive bridge game over the whole weekend, but on the other hand it meant there would be no undecided hours of nothing to do and the kind of boredom that seemed to endanger their happiness. The tournament was set up, and it was decided to play at a different house each night, just for variety.

On Friday morning Andy called Pat.

"Got any time this weekend?" He sounded as if he'd never been away, and she longed to see him.

"Oh, Andy, I'd love to see you," she said. "But this weekend is all tied up. Tim made plans for every night."

"How farsighted," he commented. "Suppose I make a plan for Christmas? Could we make it stick?"

Pat laughed. "I'd like to, Andy, I really would. It's been so long since we could talk about things."

"I'm getting tickets for *Playgirl* this weekend," he said.

"I'll let you know what night they come through for. I ordered them yesterday, and they'll be for some night during Christmas holidays. If you want to see it."

"But of course I want to see it! Oh, I've wanted to ever since it opened in Chicago. Andy, I'd love it!"

"Well, don't count on anything, but I'll let you know about the date as soon as the tickets come."

"I'll go any night you get tickets for," she promised. "I'm really sorry about this weekend, Andy. But if you could come out during the day I'd be free today or Saturday."

"I'm tied up both days, and I'm going back at noon on Sunday. Oh, well, I didn't really think you'd have any time, but I did want to talk to you. How's Tim? Steady as ever?"

"More than ever," she said, convincing herself as she always did with this reassurance.

He laughed sardonically. "If he lets his girl go out with me I question his judgment. But I'll take the girl if she'll go."

"We're still free to date other people," Pat said. "You *will* call at Christmas, then?"

"Sure. I might even write, although I'm not a very good letter writer."

"So I noticed."

"But I think about you all the time."

"Oh, sure, I *know* you do!"

At the sarcasm in her voice he laughed aloud.

"Same old Pat! Be good, sweet maid, and let who will be happy!"

He hung up, his last words sounding warningly in her ear, and she thought how much she would have enjoyed seeing him. But this weekend — she shook her head. Not now. By Christmas things should be more dependable.

The holiday weekend seemed long and dragging in spite of the bridge tournament, and Pat was divided between wishing she had given one night to Andy and being glad she hadn't, since she felt she had better be with Tim as much as possible. Ed was fun, but she would have liked to see him more devoted to Betty. Watching him closely, she was forced to conclude that Betty was just the home-town girl to him, the one he spent his time with when he was not at school.

And Betty, who treated him with an assurance and a possessiveness that Pat felt was miscalculated, told Pat, alone upstairs in the middle of the evening, that she wasn't so sure she loved Ed any more. They had a philosophical discussion on the aspects of love, and Pat was reassured, although still shaken: Betty wanted someone very different from either Tim or Ed.

" Someday you'll look up, and there he'll be," Pat promised.

" I'm watching."

Laughing, they went down to join the boys again. It was the last night of the tournament, and Tim was elated to discover that his score was high and Betty was second.

But it had not been, after all, that much fun, Pat thought, watching him and Betty. She was not going to play bridge this way again. Tim was too serious about it. Like her study habits, he thought her bridge could be improved if she concentrated. She had tried and she was glad now that the weekend was over and she could go back to studying. Exams began in one more week.

~

She passed her examinations with C in every subject. For the grades in English and geology, she could thank Tim, she knew, and she was truly grateful to him for pulling her through. She was disappointed that her courses in the School of Speech were no better. The subjects were dull; how could anyone expect her to get excited about "Elements of Voice and Diction" and "Fundamentals of Speech"? All she wanted to do was to act in plays, work with plays, talk about the theater, look at plays, study acting techniques.

A nagging conscience reminded her that if she were as good as she thought she was, she would be getting top grades at least in her field of concentration. She ignored this nagging, but she felt uneasy about her mediocre showing, and it did not help to learn that Betty Donnell had gotten two A's and two B's. Tim had enormous respect for high grades: to him they represented a good job well done. And Pat found herself driven, by some perverse reaction, to tell him Betty's grades when she would have preferred that he knew nothing about them.

However, the fall quarter was ended, vacation was upon them, and there was no schoolwork to be done for two whole, long, heavenly weeks. Connie was coming home in two days, and that meant, Pat remembered with a quickening of her emotions, that Andy would be home again too. He had not written, but that did not surprise her — as he had said, he was not a good letter writer. But she did want to see him.

Andy called her on Sunday of Christmas week at ten o'clock in the morning.

"Andy! When did you get in? I can't wait to see you."

"I'll bet you've been thinking of me day and night," he

said, and she knew exactly how his mouth twisted down with the sarcasm. "I noticed all that mail piled up in my box."

"Well, I wrote whenever you did. My box wasn't overflowing, either."

"There wasn't too much to say, after I talked to you at Thanksgiving. But I was thinking of you — more than you know."

"That's a great comfort. It would be even more comforting if I did know."

"I thought I'd come out to Allandale this afternoon, but I wanted to be sure you'd be free."

"Certainly I'll be free," Pat said promptly. "Around three?"

"I'll be there."

Tim had not said he would be busy on Sunday afternoon, but for the past few weeks he had not come over till evening. Pat was glad it worked out this way, but she dialed his number to make sure there would be no misunderstanding.

"Hi, darling. How are you this morning?"

"Fine." He sounded sleepy. "What are you doing up at this ungodly hour?"

"I'm going to church in fifteen minutes. Are you going with me?"

"Not today, honey. I just climbed out of bed. I couldn't possibly get ready in time."

"I'm going to be busy this afternoon. Are you coming over tonight?"

"Why, certainly. I was planning to come this afternoon too. What are you doing?"

"I'm going to see Andy this afternoon. He just got in

93

from Mead, and I want to hear all about it."

There was a silence, and she could almost hear Tim's thoughts racing around a track, colliding, clashing.

"Andy? That dope? What are you seeing him for?"

"Because I like him, Tim. I expect to see him several times during vacation."

"You do, huh? When?"

"I'll let you know, but it will be nights when we don't have a regular date. He wants to take me to a show."

"Well, I'll see you tonight, and we can talk about it then."

He sounded upset, she thought with some satisfaction as she put down the telephone. There had been times in the past few weeks when she had thought he was taking too much for granted, possibly (only possibly) losing interest, not quite as much in love as he had been last year.

The trouble was that, knowing she was going with Tim, no other boy on campus would ask her out, and Tim had no competition after Andy went away. It was healthy for him to be reminded that other boys might be interested in her, that she could have fun with someone else.

Andy arrived at three, running up the steps and punching the bell authoritatively.

"Hi, ugly!" he said happily.

"Same old clown," Pat retorted, giggling in spite of herself. "I thought you'd change, but I guess that's too much to hope for."

"What improvements could you ask for? Just speak and the world is yours."

"Come on in. Oh, Andy, it's such fun to see you again!"

He sat down and looked at her critically.

94

"You haven't changed either, and I'm satisfied, which is more than *you* could say. I liked you the way you were, and you're still that way."

"I am so satisfied," she protested. "Can't you take a joke?"

"I've taken it." He got up restlessly and prowled around the living room. "I didn't realize how far away Mead was. We've got time to make up, girl."

"Let's get started. Sit down and tell me all about your girls at Mead."

"Dozens." He snapped his fingers. "Different one every night. Each one prettier than the last. All mad about me. What else do you want to know about them?"

"How about the plays?"

He sat down then, and talked. He'd had one lead, he'd worked on another play. He was more convinced than ever that he wanted to specialize in theater work, but he was satisfied to get his liberal arts work done first.

"I've got tickets for *Playgirl* for next Friday," he said. "Can you go that night?"

"I'd love to! I've heard about that show for ages. Oh, Andy, it will be wonderful."

"Good. Friday night, then. And there are a couple of other shows I wanted to see this vacation. I'll get tickets for any night I can get them, and we'll see all of them."

When he had gone, she sat and thought about him. With Andy she could do so many things she wanted to do. Of course she would go to all the shows with him. Tim would just have to accept the fact that if he didn't take her to the theater, she would go with someone else.

When she told Tim about her Friday night date with Andy he was outraged.

"But that's the night of the Christmas dance — didn't you think of that?"

"You hadn't mentioned it, so I didn't," she snapped.

"But we've gone for two years! I took it for granted we'd go this year."

"You take too much for granted. When we have a date I expect to hear about it ahead of time."

He looked sulky. "If you're going to date Andy this vacation, I'm going to find somebody else," he said moodily. "I'm not sitting at home waiting for you to be free."

"But, Tim, of course you should date someone else," she tried to placate him. Inwardly his jealousy pleased her — this was the reassurance she needed that he was not becoming too sure for her.

"I don't like this running around," he grumbled. "First thing you know you'll find someone else —"

"Not a chance, darling! We're in love — you know that."

"Only you can't resist a date with Andy when he comes to town."

"I can't resist seeing a wonderful show when I get an invitation," she corrected him. "Oh, Tim, if we'd just do some of these things together, we'd have so much more fun."

"You might," he said obstinately. "But I sure as anything wouldn't have any fun at all. We'll just have to find something we can both enjoy, and — well, we both like dancing. Why do you have to go to a show on the night we could be dancing?"

"That happens to be the only night he could get tickets," Pat said, tired of the argument. "After all, this show has been sold out for weeks ahead, and he wrote for these tickets at Thanksgiving. I wish you wouldn't be

mad about it, Tim. It makes everything so uncomfortable."

"I'm not mad," Tim said, in a forbearing tone. "It just
happens that I also have tickets for this dance. I guess I'll
take Betty. She might like to go."

This threat was calculated to give Pat pause. But not
even for that would she consider missing this play.

"Ed ought to be in town," she remarked. "How about
Connie?"

"Mike is taking her," Tim reminded Pat. "We could
have doubled with them. Why don't you let Andy take
someone else to the show?"

"Because I want to go out with Andy," Pat said, getting
annoyed. "You find another girl. It would be good if you
did go out with someone else for a change."

11

For Christmas Tim gave Pat the nicest present he had ever given her — a very handsome compact.

"Oh, Tim, how beautiful!" she breathed, when she opened it on Christmas Eve after the family had scattered. "Oh, I've never had such a beautiful compact! I love it! How did you know what I wanted?"

"I guess I ought to know what you need by now," he grinned, pleased at her delight. "It came from Sinclair's," he added, wanting her to know he had gone to the finest specialty shop in town for her gift.

"I know! Oh, I appreciate this terribly, Tim. You shouldn't have spent so much money, but I love it."

"It's fun spending money for something for you," he said, somewhat surprisingly, and she glanced at him, sparkling. "Remember last year when we limited ourselves? But I love to spend money on you, and this was fun."

She gave him a wallet that she knew he had always wanted.

"When we're married," she said, as she did whenever she could bring it up, "we can give each other things for the house. If I were collecting things for a hope chest, you could give me those, even now. What would you like to collect for our home?"

In spite of the pleasure of the holiday and the delight in their gifts, Tim looked oddly uncomfortable. He laughed as if Pat's question was a hilarious joke.

"The first thing I'm concerned about is collecting a bank account," he said. "We can worry about details when we're closer to the deadline."

Pat ignored any implications in his words. The only way she could fight her occasional anxiety about Tim and herself was to act as if it were baseless, as if she had imagined things, as if she were even more certain than ever.

"If we had some idea of the kind of apartment we were going to live in," she said, as if he had answered her question differently, "perhaps we could begin to plan. It's going to take time anyway, to get everything we want. We ought to get started sometime. Why don't we go around and look at apartments before school begins again?"

"Oh, it's much too soon," said Tim, looking harried. "Even if we saw something we liked we couldn't do anything about it. By the time we wanted it, it would be gone."

She could not ignore the fact that he had not said "by next summer," and she changed the subject, trying to forget it as quickly as possible.

"Did you get a date for the Christmas dance?"

"Didn't I tell you? I'm taking Betty."

"I thought Ed was home."

"He is. But he hadn't asked her for the date, and she gave it to me."

"Well —"

He glanced at her with a teasing grin. "Your man is

99

here, and you're going out with someone else that night. What's the difference?"

She was suddenly tempted to tell Tim that she would break the date with Andy if he would break his date with Betty. But the thought of spending the evening dancing with Tim did not tempt her as much as the idea of sitting in the theater with Andy. And *Playgirl* was the kind of show no one would miss if she had a chance to go.

"It's a little different for me," she said slowly. "This play is so special. If you were willing to take me to it, I'd break any date for you. But I've got to see it, and Andy wants to take me — and we can go to a dance almost any time."

"Sure." Tim was understanding. "I'm glad you're going to have a chance to see it. I know I couldn't take a theater evening. I just don't like to sit around looking at other people do things. I guess the only thing I really don't like is Andy taking you."

She laughed, reassured again. "Don't worry about Andy," she said. "You probably aren't ever going to like theater people and I always am. We're just going to have to have different sets of friends, besides the ones we both like."

His mouth drooped forlornly.

"I wish I liked the things you like," he muttered. "I wish I could spend money the way you want to spend it. I wish we liked more of the same things."

Fear beat with frightened wings in her heart, and she laid her hand quickly on his and held it close.

"It isn't important," she implored. "It really isn't, Tim. I'll still break that date with Andy if you feel bad about it."

"I'd feel worse if you broke it," he assured her. "You

go ahead and have a wonderful time."

As if to make up for something, neither one of them was quite sure what, Tim called her more often, saw her more often, paid her more constant attention the next few days. He was with her most of Christmas Day, he came in again the next day before he went to work, he called her at suppertime, he spent the evenings with her sitting at home talking with the folks.

By the time Andy came for her on Friday night Pat was guiltily aware of a sense of release and excitement. She chattered happily on the way downtown, and within the first mile they were so engrossed in theater talk that Andy almost missed a red light, screeching to a halt halfway into the intersection.

The show was as good as its reviews, dramatic, tense, humorous. Pat was so much absorbed in the production that she forgot about Andy until the intermission.

" Like it? " he asked, as they walked out to the lobby.

" It's wonderful," she said. " I'm so impressed I can hardly believe it. And really, I didn't think it could be as good as it is."

" That's my feeling," he agreed. " What do you think of the lead? She's supposed to be not quite as good as the New York lead, but I saw this in New York a year ago, and I think she's almost better."

They talked until the lights blinked to signal them back to their seats.

When the show was over and they had applauded eleven curtain calls, Pat moved slowly up the aisle beside Andy, feeling as if she was in a dream. It was hard to bring herself back to reality, to realize that the play was over and she was in the world again. They moved slowly and silently, each wrapped in thought. About them the audience talked and laughed as they pushed up the aisle toward the street doors.

Out on the street Pat stared at the bright lights, the traffic crowding past, the people. Beside her Andy said, "Let's find a good pizza place."

The pizza was rich and hot, the coffee black and heartening.

"I'd love to be in that play sometime," Pat said, daydreaming still.

As they went out to the car to go home, Pat said, surprised at herself: "I hadn't realized how much I've missed this kind of thing, Andy. This evening has meant more than I can ever tell you."

"You shouldn't miss this kind of thing," Andy said reproachfully. "When it means so much to you, you ought to do everything you can, now while you're young. You need it. It's important."

They parked in front of the Marlowe house, still talking.

"I think you're mistaken about Tim," Andy said flatly. "I just can't see him and you together. He isn't the man."

"But he is," Pat insisted. "We're going to get married next summer. It's all planned. We're very much in love."

Andy looked ironic. "How come you're out with me and he's out with some other girl? That doesn't add up."

Then he amended his remark. "Of course, I can see how you're out with me, because not only am I irresistible, but I can offer you theater besides. But Tim — he shouldn't be interested in anyone else, if he's planning to marry you."

"He isn't, not really," Pat defended Tim. "He'd been planning to go to this dance, and when I made this date with you, because I had forgotten all about the dance — he

102

hadn't mentioned it to me — he wanted to go, even if I couldn't. And the girl who went with him is my best friend, so I know everything is all right. I'd rather have him take Betty than someone I didn't know."

"I still think there're about six fallacies in this arrangement," Andy contended. "In the first place, if you're going to get married, you both ought to be going steady and not seeing anyone else. If you can't stand that much of his company, you shouldn't be talking about marrying him."

"Oh, we've planned this for almost two years," Pat said. "But you can't concentrate exclusively for so long. We're just passing the time."

"Thank you *kindly*," Andy said, with a glance that gave her a sense of panic for fear he was permanently offended. "So the next fallacy is that you're in love with Tim. You aren't really, but you don't know it. The whole thing is a habit with you. Why don't you cut loose and enjoy yourself?"

She shook her head, determined not to listen to his argument.

"You don't understand, Andy. Don't get mad about it, but try to understand."

"In the third place," he went on, as if she hadn't spoken, "so you're in love now, you say, and you're going to get married. How long do you think it's going to last, when there isn't anything you like to do together?"

"Oh, we'll find lots of things we'll want to do when we're married and have a home and raise a family," Pat said, with a sense of repeating herself.

"That's another fallacy," he jeered. "You're making a mistake, and you're determined to make it, and no one can tell you anything."

103

"But it can't be a mistake," Pat argued. "Why, I couldn't live without Tim. I wouldn't know what to do without him. I'd die, that's all."

He glanced at her keenly and then away.

"If that's how it is," he said, accepting her words without necessarily believing them, "I'm not going to see you again. I wouldn't want to be responsible for any trouble that might come up. And I think when people see too much of each other *and* too much of everyone else, including your best friend, there's going to be trouble. Count me out."

"But I don't want to count you out!" Pat cried. And then she stopped, knowing that her arguments were foolish and Andy's were not.

"Well, don't cry about it." He sounded gruff. "Go along and play your way, and if the game blows up in your face, come and tell me about it. But as long as you feel this way about Tim, I'm not going to take you out any more. If I'd known how it was last summer, I wouldn't even have seen you this winter. I didn't really think you meant it then. But I'm not a poacher."

She turned away and opened the door and got out. Andy joined her and took her up to the door. She turned and looked up at him.

"This has still been one of the most wonderful evenings I've ever had, even if I am in love with the wrong man," she said. "Thank you a great deal, Andy. And someday I would like to talk about the theater with you again."

"That's O.K.," he said. "I could fall in love, and there's no use looking for trouble. I've got lots of other things on my mind. If you want to write me a letter sometime, I might answer it — if I'm not too busy. In the meantime, you hoe your own little row and let me know someday how the barley grows."

He turned away abruptly and ran lightly down the steps. Pat stood in the open door and watched the car pull away. He didn't even wave to her, and she stood watching the red taillights until they disappeared. Then she turned and went into the house, feeling as if she was going to cry and trying not to notice.

ANDY HAD SAID he would get tickets for a couple more shows during the Christmas holidays, but Pat did not hear from him again. Evidently he had meant what he said about not seeing her again while she felt as she did about Tim. She thought for a long time about the evening they had spent together at *Playgirl*, searching through old newspapers for reviews, agreeing happily with one, disagreeing violently with the other. She wanted to call Andy and talk to him again, but something warned her that the conversation would not be satisfactory. After his ultimatum when he had left her that night, he must be the one to search her out.

Deprived of such conversation, she felt irritated with Tim because she could not talk to him.

He came over the night after the play, as usual. His coming was so customary, so much a part of her life now, that she always felt that something was missing when he was late, or, rarely, prevented from coming. And yet she could not look forward to seeing him, because there was nothing, really, to talk about. While she waited for him on Saturday she thought again about this difference between them, and asked herself again how really important this lack of common interest might be. Shakespeare had said something about a "marriage of true minds." She felt that with Andy she was in tune. With Tim, something was missing, something was out of key. And yet, when she thought of breaking with Tim, everything seemed to stop — her thoughts, her heart, even her breathing for a moment.

She was so used to him, she knew what to expect with him, she was accustomed to his attention and devotion (although that devotion was less adoring than it had once been), all her thoughts were keyed to him. And underlying all her other reactions was the sense of panic: If I didn't have Tim, whom could I rely on?

Andy? She thought, Well, perhaps. But she knew him so little compared to Tim. The idea of getting so well acquainted with another man was frightening, so much time had gone by. She had closed the door to any other future for so long. How could she know what to expect from anyone else?

This panicky reaction she never acknowledged, even to herself. But it was there, tightening the bonds, bulwarking the determination she expressed so often to marry Tim next summer, or anyway, soon.

The door opened and Tim walked in, as the family had long ago invited him to do.

"Hi, honey. How was the play?" He kissed her in the manner of a home-coming husband.

"Oh, it was wonderful." She felt herself going all starry-eyed in reminiscence, as she took his hand to lead him into the living room.

"That's nice. I'm glad you could go." Tim's tone dismissed the subject without further comment, and Pat felt a little irritation sprouting again, an irritation that was becoming so familiar that she hardly noticed it any longer or tried to conceal it.

"I am too," she said. "How was the dance? Did you have fun?"

"Oh, yes. We had a great time. Betty's quite a girl, isn't she?"

"I guess so. What about her Ed?"

He shrugged. "That situation seems to be vague. She's going out with him tonight, I guess. I don't know what he was doing last night."

He sat down and picked up the financial section of the evening paper, studied it for a few minutes while Pat hunted for the crossword puzzle, and then looked over the top of it.

"Did I tell you I've been reading up on the stock market?"

"No! What on earth for?"

"Well, it's fascinating. I think I've got a new hobby. Look here, I'll show you what I'm doing. This is something we could have fun with together. Have you got a pencil and paper around?"

Pat found some yellow paper in her mother's study, a pencil, a magazine to put under the paper, and sat down beside Tim to hear about his new discovery.

"Mom's Uncle Joe — that was my grandfather's brother — made about a million dollars in the stock market, and when he died last year he left Mom some stock. Well, she just got it last week, and I went with her to the broker to figure out what to do about it, and she found that Great-Uncle Joe bought some of it for ten bucks a share and now it's worth a hundred, and another he got for five bucks has been split three times, and the ten shares

108

he started with is now eighty shares, and every one of them is worth twenty bucks."

He looked up at Pat, his eyes sparkling.

" So I says: ' Where has this been all my life? Not only is it a good way to make some money, but it's interesting! ' The broker laughed like crazy and said: ' The market has fooled some of the experts. But who knows? Sometimes it's the amateurs that have all the luck,' so he lent me a couple of books about it. And, boy, is it fascinating! "

" You mean we might get a couple of thousand dollars in the market quick? "

" Could be," Tim said, dreaming aloud.

Pat sat up straight. "How much did you say we had to have to get married? "

" Oh, five thousand or so."

"Tim! " she wailed. " You said fifteen hundred would be enough."

" I forgot about inflation."

" How much have we got now? "

He grinned at her. " Who's saving this money? "

" Well, I've saved some," she said defensively, thinking of the fifteen dollars she had hidden in her dresser drawer. " But I had to use a lot for my clothes for college. Mother said I should get them. But after all, I can use them when I get married."

" I've got about a thousand now," he said comfortably. " But there's lots of time. So one of the books tells you how to buy and sell on paper for practice, and that's what I'm doing. I invested a thousand dollars in Uranium, Ltd., at $47 a share. I got twenty shares, so that was 940 bucks, plus commission makes it $950." He wrote out the figures as he talked.

"Tim, you didn't take your savings and buy stocks with it, did you?"

"No, no, no, of course not; now pay attention to what I'm telling you. This is a practice account. I do it all on paper. I start with a fixed amount of capital, and I used $1,000 because that's what I'd have if I wanted to do it for real. Then I keep a bookkeeping record like this"—he sketched out for her the columns for dates, purchase price, number of shares, commission, selling price, and balance —"then I watch the prices in the paper from day to day. When I think it's time to sell, I record it here and take the money and buy something else. See how it works?"

"Like a game," Pat said intelligently. "Like solitaire — something you can play by yourself?"

"That's right. But you can play it with me. It's more fun when you can talk about it."

How true, she agreed silently. Anything you liked to do was more fun when you could talk about it with someone.

"What is Uranium, Ltd., selling for tonight?" she asked, trying to be interested, although it seemed like a slow-moving game to her.

"47½," he said proudly. "So I've made ten bucks in a week's time. One broker thinks it's going to a hundred before summer. But I'd be satisfied with 98. That would double my price and pay commissions besides. When it gets up there I'll sell and we'll buy something else. Let me see that financial page again."

He pored over the stock listings, reading occasionally the names of stocks that might be a good investment when he switched out of Uranium, and Pat listened, dutifully trying to be fascinated and feeling that the whole thing was like shadowboxing. What was the use of spending your time playing a game like this, when it was only a game?

"It's more than just a game," Tim pointed out to her. "It's getting acquainted with the market, without risking your money until you know what it's all about. Now, take this tobacco stock: it's jumped in the last three weeks, about twenty points. But tonight it's off three. If I'd bought it three weeks ago, I'd have a nice profit. If I bought it now, who knows?"

He went over the columns of stock listings again, pencil in hand, marking stocks he was going to find out about, frowning thoughtfully, and occasionally throwing out a remark like, "Perhaps this would be a good time to buy steel," and "You can't buy and sell too often — the commissions would eat up all your gains," and "Boy, if I'd just gotten Jewel Tea last month. It's up ten points already!" Pat worked in a desultory fashion on her crossword puzzle, interrupting him now and then to ask about a word, and getting no help. At nine she looked at her watch.

"There's a wonderful TV program on now, Tim. I've been waiting all week to see this."

"You go ahead," he said comfortably. "I've got an idea about this market that I want to try and dope out. Maybe I'd get farther if I could afford to have more than one stock at a time."

Pat went out to the TV room in a frame of mind divided between resentment that Tim never wanted to do anything she wanted to do and guilt that she could not bring herself to participate wholeheartedly in something in which he was deeply interested. What was the use of having a date with him, when he spent it in one room study-

111

ing the stock market while she was in another room looking at TV?

But there were too many nights in Christmas vacation. Even Tim could not spend every night working out problems about the stock market, especially with his limited commitment (on paper). The game was slow, as Pat had recognized. She asked questions, she tried to talk about it intelligently. But it was remote and vague to her, and Tim, sensing her lack of real interest, could not bring his hobby to life for her.

They went to a movie when Tim agreed that they might as well, since there was nothing else to do. They double-dated with Mike and Connie once, they double-dated with Betty and Ed, whom Pat found she definitely did not like. Time dragged, and she looked forward eagerly to getting back in school, when she could spend some of her time at the house with the girls.

Back on campus, she confidently expected things to be running smoothly again. What they both needed, she told herself, was to have more to do, more people around, not to be able to concentrate on each other so much. The routine of the school quarter provided a good framework for getting together. Within that framework they met at the Grill at ten thirty every morning. This quarter several of Pat's sorority sisters met with them, and Betty was always there. Pat and Tim met for lunch again, as they had last quarter, and now Pat felt obliged to include Betty. She wasn't quite sure why she did, but Tim seemed to enjoy Betty, and Pat felt that having someone else with them seemed to provide the gaiety and relaxation that eluded them when they were alone. Besides, Tim was always in a better mood when Betty was along.

112

There always seemed to be so much to talk about when they were a threesome or a foursome. And Betty could scold Tim, tell him hard truths about himself, threaten him that she wouldn't put up with what Pat put up with for one minute. From Betty, Tim took these lectures with a teasing grin, and of course Betty always smiled back, letting him know that she thought he was a pretty wonderful person in spite of his faults, and Pat was lucky to have him.

Tim was happy in these sessions, and Pat could relax in the belief that this was the way life would be when they were married and could have friends with them in their own home. And although she was inclined to be uneasy over Tim's very gaiety when Betty was with them, she was sorry when Betty could not join them.

As initiation approached, two weeks after school opened in the second quarter, Tim became more and more downcast about her getting initiated; and during the week before initiation she could not see him at all — this was part of the hazing routine. She was even instructed to drive herself to school daily. And being thus prevented from seeing him, she missed him hideously.

Absence does make the heart grow fonder, she thought, reassured to know that an ancient adage had been proved true. The adage about the rough path of true love reassured her too, except that she and Tim had never had a rough path. One of her sorority sisters had said that every love affair she had ever known had broken up at least once in its course to the altar, and if Pat and Tim didn't have a good, rousing fight, how could Pat tell if they really cared for each other? Another sister, Julie Lombard, illustrated this convincingly. Her man, Ted Stokely, had

113

broken with her last summer, and over the Christmas holidays just past he had returned, and within a week had given her a ring and set a date for their marriage next summer. Pat gave some thought to fighting with Tim over her initiation. But in the end he was only sorrowful, not angry, and she felt that it would do no good to pick a fight deliberately.

Initiation, with all the girls in white evening gowns, the room candlelit and filled with flowers and soft music, all the girls tearful with the majesty of the ceremony, was the most beautiful experience Pat had ever had. She felt herself growing at that moment, becoming unexpectedly older, reaching for standards of personality and achievement that the Alpha sorority represented. And she did not think of Tim once, even when she glanced above her candle across the circle to where Betty was standing.

The ceremony was over, she was wearing her sorority mother's pin (she kept feeling it to be sure it was really true, that it was still there), the girls kissed the new initiates, the initiates kissed each other, and Pat felt that no matter what happened, she was part of a loyal, understanding group that would be important to her the rest of her life. She felt like a different girl from the one who had walked into the room tonight, and she expected confidently that friends and teachers would recognize the change. Then the doors were opened, and banished boy friends arrived to pick up the girls.

"Hi, darling!" Tim came through the door while her back was turned.

"Oh, Tim, look at my pin! It was the most beautiful evening! And it's so good to see you again!"

"I'll say! It's been a long week. Ready to leave now?"

114

He kissed her as if a congratulatory kiss was expected, she waved to the remaining sisters, and they went out to Tim's car.

Halfway home she turned to him, remembering something important that had slipped her mind during the excitement of the past week.

"Tim, did I tell you? I got a part in *A Doll's House*! I'm so thrilled. They hardly ever cast freshmen, and I never expected to get into a play here this year. It's a small part, but it has lots of possibilities. I can't wait to begin rehearsals!"

Tim looked less than delighted.

"That's fine, dear. But won't rehearsals take an awful lot of time?"

She bounced on the front seat in her enthusiasm, not noticing Tim's lack of excitement.

"We began rehearsals a couple of days ago, and after this week we'll be working at night. Will you study on campus and drive me home?"

He drew down his black eyebrows in an unhappy frown.

"I hate to study on campus, Pat. You know that. I can't concentrate at that library. Why do you have to get involved in things that keep you down here at night?"

"You don't have to study on campus if you don't want to," she said coldly. "I just thought you'd like to pick me up. Because otherwise I won't have a chance to see you at all on the nights we're rehearsing. I can always drive myself down and home again, so the ride isn't important. But I thought we could have a little extra time together that way."

His face, eyes steadily fixed on the road ahead, was impassive, but he nodded.

" O.K., O.K. It's only a ten-minute run. I'll come down and get you. When do you get through? "

" Probably around ten," she said. " I'd love it if you did, Tim. I miss you so much when I don't see you."

She threw that in to make him feel better. She didn't want him to think she was interested in his giving her transportation alone — she really did want to see him. When she stopped to think, which she did as seldom as possible, she knew her wanting to see him was not because she was really missing him, but because she had this uneasy feeling all the time now that things were not really the way they were last summer, or even last fall. She felt as if he were slipping away, and that the more she kept him by her side the more sure she could feel about him.

IN THE FOURTH WEEK of the quarter rehearsals were beginning to run later. The girls who lived on campus were signing out for eleven o'clock instead of ten. Mrs. Marlowe protested Pat's late hours, and Pat said: "But, Mother, there's nothing I can do. The play is opening next Friday night, and it's nowhere near ready. Mr. Gwynn has to work late. Besides, Tim always brings me home. You don't need to worry about that."

Mrs. Marlowe didn't need to worry, but Pat herself was beginning to. Tim evidently did not enjoy running down to the campus every night in the week to fetch her home. She tried to tell herself it was all imagination, that of course he enjoyed being with her as much as she wanted to be with him. But the week of final rehearsals precipitated an outspoken sulky protest.

She told Tim that he needn't come this week before eleven, and at eleven on Tuesday night Tim arrived. The weather was bitter cold, and Eloise was balky. By the time he got to Evanston, snow was falling in a light skiddy covering.

Rehearsal was still going on. The director had discovered a snag in the third act, and called for a rerun of the whole act at ten forty-five. Pat felt that he was absolutely right — the third act was very rough; but the rest of the cast were irritated and tired, and tempers were running high.

She watched in the wings, waiting for her entrance, when, looking into the auditorium, she saw Tim come in and sit down in the back row. Her first thought was that she was glad he could see the play. Some moments later she began to worry about his getting impatient. The work went on and on, and Pat's mind was divided between the few lines she had to deliver and wishing she could speak to Tim, wondering whether he was really upset about the delay.

She could not see, in the shadows of the house, the expression on his face. Tim rarely showed annoyance, and from the wings all she could see was a kind of tired patience. She told herself she would never have the nerve to tell him to come early enough to see part of the rehearsal, but it was good for him, and she was glad he had this chance to watch it. She still hoped that if he saw enough dramatic work, watched the director working out the fine distinctions in the scenes, was exposed to this experience for a long enough time, that someday he would find himself interested in spite of himself.

Before the rehearsal ended she was tired herself, and beginning to get edgy with delay. When she joined Tim it was five minutes after twelve.

"For Pete's sake!" he exploded. "What's the idea of keeping everyone around till this time of the night?"

"Darling, I'm so tired!" She leaned against him for comfort. "I don't know what went wrong tonight. Mr. Gwynn was beside himself. Absolutely nothing seemed to go right,

118

and dress rehearsal is next Thursday. But I'm terribly sorry you had to wait. I had no idea — "

" I was right in the middle of this assignment that's due tomorrow, and I broke off because I thought you'd be ready by eleven o'clock, and now I've got an hour's work to do when I get home. And it's snowing."

She glanced at his face. He looked furious, and her heart misgave her. He had been irritable lately, but he had never been really angry with her. She withdrew, trying to think of the best way to soothe him. The snow was partly to blame — he hated driving in snow. Instinct told her that if she betrayed anger in turn it would only solidify his exasperation, and they might quarrel seriously. Last spring Tim had been frantic at the suggestion of a serious quarrel. Now she was the one who was disturbed.

" How did you spend the evening? " she changed the subject. " Did you get your math done? "

" I went over to study with Betty. I told her in class today that we'd better do this next assignment together, it's so tough. But we couldn't get finished."

She said nothing, while her thoughts ranged over the implications in his words.

" Darling," she said plaintively, " I wish you'd stay with me through rehearsals. I'm only on in two acts for a couple of minutes, and I could sit in the back of the room with you the rest of the time. We could study together."

" Nope," he said positively. "I'm not going to sit through any of these rehearsals. It's enough to come down and get you when they're over."

" I'm sorry," she said, moving close to him again. " I really am, Tim. You don't have to pick me up if you don't want to. The only reason I suggested it was because I knew I wouldn't see you otherwise, and I miss you so much when we aren't together."

"I miss you, too, honey." He pulled in to the curb in front of her house and parked and took her in his arms. "I get so upset about these things that seem to take you away from me. There was all that initiation nonsense, and now this play. And when this is finished, there'll be something else. Sometimes I wonder —"

"Nothing means as much to me as you do." She lifted her head and kissed him. "Darling, don't *worry* so much. I'm only doing this because it's part of my work in the School of Speech, and I wouldn't let it come between us for anything."

He held her tight. "But it does come between us; there isn't anything either one of us can do about it."

"You could learn to like it," she muttered stubbornly.

He released his hold a little. "You could learn to forget it."

She spoke quickly to avoid thinking about the alternatives implied in his words.

"Darling, don't *worry* about it. The play will be over in two more weekends, and after that I won't be in another one for a long time. Perhaps not this year."

"That's good."

He sounded as if he appreciated her efforts to comfort him, but as if he were not convinced. Getting out of the car, he walked around and opened Pat's door.

"Only good thing in this business is that I can see you till one o'clock in the morning," he joked. "You know your dad wouldn't let us have a date till one in the middle of the week otherwise."

She was glad he could make a joke out of it, and she

made her good-night kiss a special effort to show him she loved him more than ever.

The trouble was, she had to make the special effort. She believed, when she watched Tim walk back to the car through the snow, that the shadow of a rift had disappeared again. What she did not realize was that she was beginning to use their love-making for special purposes: to cheer him up when he was melancholy, to reassure him when he was pessimistic about their future, to persuade him that she was deeply in love with him and that he was passionately, single-mindedly in love with her. Making love now meant that she wanted to kiss and caress him not only because she loved him, but because there was some misunderstanding that must be smoothed over, and making love as and when Tim wanted to was the easiest way to keep him content.

When they went out Sunday night everything seemed to be normal, " the way it used to be," Pat said, unaware that she was admitting everything was no longer that way. They went over to the Davises' to visit with his parents, and Pat played Scrabble with Mrs. Davis while Tim tinkered with his hi-fi set in happy solitude. Pat was fond of Mrs. Davis since she had come to know her, and counted herself as one of the family. She knew the Davis home as well as her own — there had been many Saturdays when she had cleaned the kitchen for Mrs. Davis while she worked at the hardware store, or washed supper dishes after she had dined there with Tim. She had been included in family parties when an aged uncle or a distant aunt had come to visit, and had helped to prepare the guest room or bake the cookies for an evening party. She loved to spend time there, feeling that the more accustomed his parents

121

became to having her around, the more stable was the future. So now she played Scrabble, laughing at the occasional joke that Mr. Davis offered, listening with half an ear to the TV program he enjoyed.

At ten o'clock, because they had classes the next day, Pat and Tim left. She felt more deeply, calmly happy than she had for some time. It seemed as if all their differences and misunderstandings had been resolved.

In front of her house Tim took her in his arms.

"You don't have to go in for a while," he whispered. "That's why we left by ten."

She pulled away. "Tim, we've got to take it easy."

He looked at her in astonishment.

"What's the matter with you? Don't you love me any more? Don't you trust me?"

"Of course I love you, darling," she said, feeling weary that it had to be proved and asserted over and over. "But we can't go on like this indefinitely. It's getting harder all the time and — oh, I don't know. I just don't feel like being quite so —" She knew what she meant, but she didn't know quite how she wanted to say it, and she fell silent, detaching his hands and moving away from him.

"Well," he said angrily, "I guess I don't know what's going on any more. I figure if a girl doesn't want to make love, she isn't interested in a guy."

Pat leaned her head on her hand, tired and thoughtful.

"You know I love you, Tim. I've shown you that over and over. But tonight I just don't feel that way, somehow."

"Don't you feel well, honey?"

She jumped at the excuse. "I've got a headache coming on, and I feel as if I'm worn out. Maybe I've been working too hard."

She made her voice plaintive, and he dropped his annoyance and became concerned.

"You need more sleep, darling. That play has been keeping you up too many nights, when you've got classes all day."

"I'll be all right by tomorrow."

But she wasn't. There was nothing wrong with her health; she felt just fine all day long. But when she was alone with Tim she had the instinctive withdrawal that had developed on Sunday night. She simply didn't care about making love with him as she once had, although on Monday night she exerted herself to more effort, hoping that Tim was not aware of her failing interest.

Later, when he had gone, she thought about it soberly. This must be one of those things that develops when love is no longer new, when you have gotten used to someone, as she and Tim were used to each other. Besides, they had been getting pretty intense. So she was reasonable and prudent to check their emotions where she did, she told herself.

She thought, satisfied, as she fell asleep, that this was wise and commendable, that her mother would be pleased if she knew. (But, of course, you never let your mother know about these problems!) What she did not realize was that her instinct for slowing down the progress of their love-making was not due to exemplary insight and self-discipline, but rather was to waning affection.

This idea Pat would have denied with tearful vigor. She kept asserting, to him and herself and anyone else to whom she could say it, that she was deeply in love with Tim. Their plans were made, had been made for two years; they were just waiting till next summer to get married. She wondered sometimes why next summer seemed so extremely vague, so unconvincing. But it was still far away. This was February. Perhaps by May they could begin to plan for a late summer wedding. Thus she soothed any fears when they leaped up, and persuaded herself there was no reason for alarm.

The three performances of the play went off extremely well the following weekend, and Tim attended on Friday night. He brought Betty to the play, because, he explained to Pat during intermission, Betty was dying to see it and had no way to get there. Pat cast a sharp glance at Betty, who smiled at her gaily.

"I didn't know how I was going to get here," she said vivaciously. "The folks wouldn't let me have the car tonight, and I thought I was going to have to miss the performance altogether, and then Tim said as long as he had to come alone, why didn't I keep him company? It's a terrific production, Pat. I'm simply mad about it. I'd like to see all the performances."

Pat's suspicions were lulled. Perhaps with an enthusiastic companion like Betty, Tim would enjoy it more. It didn't occur to her that there could be any danger in Tim's learning in Betty's company to enjoy something he had formerly disliked.

"I'm glad you're keeping Tim company," she said warmly. "I think Mr. Gwynn has done a terrific job. The more I work with him, the more impressed I am with what he can get out of a play. Did you notice that business in the second scene, where Greg moves the clock from one side of the room to the other?"

Betty had noticed everything, and Tim agreed that everything she pointed out was interesting and important.

124

Satisfied, Pat returned to the wings for the second act, promising to meet them after the performance.

It was ridiculous that she should feel like the extra wheel later that night when they rode home together. After all, if anyone was extra, it was Betty. They went out to get something to eat before they left Evanston, and while Pat would have enjoyed being alone with Tim, with Betty she could continue talking about the play, and she told herself that Tim should pick up something from being exposed to this kind of talk.

Somewhere on the ride home Tim diverted the conversation to his paper-trading game with the stock market, and Pat felt a sharp jab of alarmed surprise to hear Betty discuss the stock market with him as knowledgeably as if she were playing the game too. They chatted for several minutes while Pat listened, realizing that this was so important to Tim that she ought to know at least as much about it as Betty seemed to. But her questions were so elementary that she felt foolish when Tim answered them, and it was apparent, when Betty answered one for her, that she was betraying herself as stupid in an area where Tim and Betty both were well informed. He must have talked a lot to Betty, Pat thought.

As Betty left them, she said to Pat, "Why don't you both come over to my house for lunch tomorrow?"

Pat looked at Tim. She had not expected to see him for lunch on Saturday, knowing that he usually worked all day and came over to her house around four.

"Can you take off that much time at noon?" she asked.

"Oh, sure," Tim said. "That would be fun, Betty. I'll pick up Pat and we'll be there — around twelve thirty?"

"Good. I've got a wonderful recipe for barbecue sauce

that I want you to taste. I think you'll like it."

"Seems to me," Pat said coolly as they drove on to her house, "that we're spending an awful lot of time with Betty lately."

"She's fun," Tim said easily, "and while you've been rehearsing I would have been pretty lonesome if she hadn't studied with me. She's a good kid."

With that Pat tried to be content. She could not shut Betty out of their lives now — she needed her too much. Tim was so cheerful when they were all together; he was inclined to be irritable when he and Pat were alone. They argued more when they were by themselves, but Betty kept the conversation turned to channels that avoided argument. Pat told herself: All men are alike. When they've got a girl, they still want to know that other girls like them. They want to feel irresistible.

She tried to give Tim that conviction of being irresistible when she kissed him good night, later. But she felt as if she were acting, she felt as if she were battling bad dreams, evanescent misty threats that would fade in tomorrow's sun.

"I love you so much," she whispered. "Tim, darling, tell me you love me."

"Of course I love you," he said.

WITH *A Doll's House* over, Pat determined that she was not going to work in another play for a long time. She made this decision with hardly a qualm: the theater was creating a gulf between herself and Tim which she could no longer ignore, and this distance between them Betty was filling much too well.

She was not jealous of Betty. She was confident that Tim was enjoying Betty only as a substitute for herself, that Betty was too loyal a friend and sorority sister to allow any feeling to develop between herself and Tim. But still, Pat knew it was not entirely wise to leave Tim alone so much, to let him become accustomed to enjoying himself without her. Something was missing, even now, and she could not put her finger on it. In an effort to repair the situation, she stayed away from the School of Speech except for required classes, she avoided her drama friends, she stayed by Tim's side as much as she could. And she talked more often about their marriage.

"When we are married," she said one night, when they were studying at her house, thinking about her wedding instead of her geology, "I want to go someplace where I've never been — like Florida, except that that might not be good in August. Do you suppose we could take a honeymoon for four weeks and go out to Colorado? "

Tim looked up from his book and then down at his hands.

"I'm deferring our marriage later than August," he said, slowly and positively. "Much later."

Pat stared at him. "But why? " she cried. "I mean — we planned to get married next summer. Why not? "

"Well, for one thing," he said without looking at her, "we're not going to have enough money. I've decided fifteen hundred isn't going to be enough for two more years of school. And you've never worked steadily — you don't know what's involved. You wouldn't be able to work part time in school and keep up all you have to do in the Speech School on the side — "

The argument was unanswerable. Pat returned silently to her book, staring at the pages without understanding them — arguments, questions flying through her mind, arguments that she answered for herself, questions that she knew were useless.

"But if we were married we'd make it work," she offered, knowing it was weak. "I could work in the hardware store with you. Your father always needs an extra clerk. Why couldn't we do it the way we planned? "

"I just don't think it's a good idea right now, dear." He sounded so mature and fatherly that she was at once reassured and secretly amused.

"You're probably right, darling," she said, suddenly determined to agree with him instead of allowing any difference to arise. He smiled at her then, and she thought with satisfaction that this agreement instead of argument must solidify their understanding.

However, doubts attacked her the next day. She kept remembering implications that she had not noticed or had ignored the night before.

Betty was lunching with them. Betty seemed to be lunching with them every day now, and Pat was annoyed but helpless. She joined them every morning at the Grill, and always Tim said, " We're eating at my house — want to come along? " or Pat felt compelled to say, " You can ride home with us if you want to," and then of course Betty stayed with them.

She was gay company, and Pat found herself laughing at Betty's remarks. Betty was still her best friend, and they could discuss the sorority sisters, problems of mutual friends, teachers, grades — Betty's grades were high, Pat's were slipping. Oh, Betty did contribute a lot of life to their lunch hours. And then there were the questions they submitted to her judgment.

Once Pat said: " Betty, Tim and I can't agree about dates. Now, what do you think? He says when he hates movies so much, it's foolish to spend a couple of dollars on a movie date when we could spend the time for free at home and put the money in the bank. And I say even a Western movie once in a while is better than nothing."

" What would you do if you didn't go to the movie? " Betty inquired judiciously.

" Tim would work on his stock market game and I'd do a crossword puzzle," Pat said, a little bitterly. " Or else I'd be looking at TV, and he doesn't like that either. Or we'd go over to his house and I'd play Scrabble with his mother while he worked on his hi-fi set."

" But you don't like Westerns," Betty pointed out, " and if he doesn't like them either, then it seems to me Tim is

129

right and you'd do better to save the money, if you're planning to get married."

The reference to their marriage dropped like a stone in a pool, without any reaction from Tim. Pat glanced at him, waiting for his smile, waiting for him to say, "See, darling, it just means we could get married sooner." But he said nothing.

Another time Tim said, "Pat says if I loved her I'd like what she likes, but she doesn't take any interest in the stock market, and I think a savings and investment program is basic for both of us."

Betty considered the argument thoughtfully, and Pat waited for her to say: "But you really ought to take an interest in something like the theater, Tim. You should broaden your mind a little." Instead she said: "It seems to me, Pat, that you really ought to get interested in Tim's hobby. After all, a man is going to have to earn the money and support the family, and if his wife doesn't care about anything he's doing to make a little extra money, it's kind of a lonesome business for him."

Pat cried, outraged at her side of the argument being neglected: "But, Betty, this business of common interests is a two-way street! We can't spend all our lives together earning and saving money. Somewhere along the way there's going to be time to spend in recreation and culture. It's just as important for Tim to learn to like something like the theater as for me to learn about money. I'd just as soon learn about the stock market — I'm interested! But he ought to be interested in my hobbies too!"

Betty did not answer. She smiled at Tim and Pat saw Tim smile back at her, as if he felt she understood him better than Pat did, and he appreciated her feeling. It was

130

like a knife in her heart, and from that moment she began to distrust Betty.

"I don't think Betty's decisions are necessarily right," she said, when they had dropped Betty for her afternoon class and were walking across campus together.

"Oh, I think she's a pretty levelheaded girl," Tim said. "After all, she's thinking of the best thing for both of us, and she knows us both pretty well."

Pat sniffed and lifted her head rebelliously. But she said nothing more, only wishing that they need see no more of Betty. But the pattern had been set. Betty was now a regular part of their luncheon hours, and once or twice when Pat had a noon appointment that forced her to eat earlier or later than Tim's noon hour, he told her casually later that he and Betty had gone to Betty's house for a hamburger.

As February advanced Pat knew that she was losing Tim.

The knowledge had grown upon her, almost without her realizing it, until she was living with it a dead weight upon her thoughts, trying with every tactic she could find to dislodge the idea, to keep him more and more closely by her side. She called him on the phone every night immediately after supper, even though there was nothing to say and she knew that he would be coming to see her at nine thirty, as he had done all year. She told him over and over how much she loved him, how much he meant to her; she told everyone, whenever she could introduce the subject, that she was meeting Tim for Coke, going home with Tim after classes, that they were going to get married. And she was clinging to Betty with an unconscious sense of self-preservation. She could talk to Betty about

131

Tim, she could ask her questions, and if she were with Betty, at least Betty and Tim would not be alone together.

"But of course Tim loves you," Betty said over and over. "He's told me so. All men hang back from getting married, when it comes right down to setting a date. I wouldn't let that worry me for one minute."

The only question Pat dared not ask Betty outright was: "What do you think of Tim, Betty? How much do you care?"

She did ask, at the Alpha house one day: "What's happened to Ed, Betty? Do you hear much from him?"

Betty shrugged with calm indifference. "Oh, he writes. But I told him long ago I wasn't waiting for him with my hands folded."

"Do you ever see Joe Simpson?"

"Not too much. I don't think Joe is going to get interested in anyone until he's through school."

"I liked Joe. He's an awfully nice kid."

"Oh, I liked him all right. He's a good bridge partner."

Pat turned away to join a crowd of girls around the piano, without replying. She was not going to invite Betty to play bridge with them again with Joe or anyone else. But when Tim suggested that they should play bridge on Saturday night, instead of going to a movie, Pat acceded without discussion. She could not very well refuse when she could offer no other entertainment that he would enjoy, and she felt trapped.

She made the most of the evening by saying as she dealt out the cards, with a warm smile at Joe, "When Tim and I are married, Joe, you must come around and see us often."

This gambit fell flat. Joe said, "I'd love to, Pat," but

neither Tim nor Betty said anything. At the end of the evening Pat stood close to Tim, her arm linked through his, as she said good night to her guests, and added: " Come back soon, kids. It was a wonderful evening."

" We'll do that," they said together.

" Well, dear," Tim kissed her, " it's so late now I won't try to come back after I run the kids home. See you tomorrow."

He ran down the steps to join Betty and Joe, and Pat turned back into the house with an empty feeling of being deserted. She knew Tim's routine: he would take Betty home and then he and Joe would go out and talk until three in the morning. Or they would take Betty with them and talk. Or would he take Joe home first?

With a heavy melancholy settling down into a headache, Pat turned out the lights and stumbled up to bed.

The worst trouble with this business was that she could no longer concentrate on her studies. During the days on campus she had an hour or two between classes when, in the first quarter, she had gone to the library or the Alpha house and studied. Now she could not isolate herself thus; she knew where Tim was every hour of the day, and she found herself wandering restlessly near his class buildings, waiting for him to come out and walk with her to the next class. She spent the morning hour in the Grill, and then part of the afternoon, because she could no longer tolerate staying alone with her books. She had to have company, friends she could talk to, other boys she could flirt with; if she could feel that half a dozen other boys liked her, even if only to have a cup of coffee with, she had a little insulation against the cold world of being alone without Tim.

She avoided students from the drama department. She was convinced now that her devotion to the theater program was in some way responsible for this precarious situation with Tim, and she was going to detach herself from the theater as much as possible. She tried out the idea on some of her sorority sisters, just for the reaction.

"I might just transfer out of Speech School next year," she suggested. "I don't know that I really want a career in the theater."

"But Pat, you're doing so well there!" her sorority mother, Julie Lombard, exclaimed. Julie was a senior in the School of Speech and noted on campus for her ability. Pat felt a twinge of nostalgia.

"I'll think about it," she offered. "I'd probably miss it. But on the other hand, it cuts out so many other things I'd like to be doing."

Julie looked at her skeptically. The sorority was well aware that far from doing "so many other things" this quarter, Pat was doing nothing at all except her studies since A Doll's House had ended.

"The trouble is," Pat elaborated, "Tim hates the theater, and I don't know whether I'll want to go on with it after we're married or not, when he feels that way."

Julie was immediately sympathetic. This clash of interests was something all girls encountered at one time or another, and they understood her problem.

"Tim's a sweetie," Julie said, and Pat's heart warmed to her. "It's one of those problems everyone has to face. I wouldn't know what to say. After all, you will have to be doing something with your mind and your time after you're married."

Pat thought about it constantly in the next weeks, so

134

constantly that she could not study for the mid-terms, and only by grace of coincidence did she manage to pass two of them with C's. The other two she failed completely. The day she heard, she was overcome with a revulsion against school, and a dreary sense of futility.

She and Tim were eating lunch together that day, with Betty, at Pat's house, and she rode up to Allandale with them in gloomy silence. Tim talked about one subject in which he had gotten B when he thought he had made an A, and Betty made a lot of conversation about her two B's and two A's, when she had expected to flunk, she claimed. Pat hated her at that moment, and said nothing, hoping they wouldn't ask about her grades.

But when lunch was finished and they sat around Pat's kitchen table drinking the last cup of coffee before they started back to the campus, Tim said, " How did you come out on your mid-terms, Pat?"

She wanted to say casually, " Oh, I got all A's," and the thought flashed through her mind that he would never know the difference if she did tell him a lie. But at the same moment, the overpowering sense of futility that had assailed her when she got her grades overwhelmed her again. What was the use of anything?

" I got two F's," she said with a debonair indifference, and then in a passion of despair she cried: " I *hate* school! I'd like to drop out and never go back. I'm not a student. I *hate* studying! "

She looked from Tim's impassive expression to Betty's eyes resting on Tim's before they met Pat's. Betty looked sympathetic, but it was the kind of sympathy you extend to a moron, a helpless idiot who can do no better.

Theater, ambition, professional aims, smothered in the

135

past weeks, were now forgotten completely. Clutching frantically and instinctively for emotional reassurance and security, Pat said with a bright optimistic expression, "Tim, if I dropped out of school and got a job next quarter, we could get married next summer."

"No, we couldn't." Tim looked at her like an adult trying to reason with a child.

"But I don't see why not!" Pat argued. "The only reason we were putting it off was financial," she asserted, trying to believe it herself. "I don't care about school. I could work from here on and we'd have plenty of money."

"That isn't, the point," Tim said frankly. "You're too young for marriage, Pat. You've got a lot to learn before I'm going to marry you."

There was a dull silence, while Pat tried to forget she had said anything.

"Well, come on." She got up hastily, wanting to change the subject, think about something else, get away from Tim's forthright statement. "Time to get back. I've got a lot of studying to do, Tim."

Thus she hoped to dispel his accusation of being too young, hoped to convince him that he was mistaken. Give her next quarter, she thought, and everything would be back to normal.

"I CAN'T imagine what is the matter with Tim," Pat said to Betty two weeks later, when they were waiting for chapter meeting on Monday night. "He's so irritable these days. We seem to fight all the time."

Betty smiled at Pat with an expression of "women must stand together in these things," and said: "That's how Ed was last Christmas. I wouldn't put up with it. I just told him I was through."

Pat studied her. "You aren't advising me to break with Tim, are you?" she asked sharply.

"Oh, no," said Betty quickly. "Not unless, of course, you feel that it's time to make an issue out of something."

"But I love him," Pat declared. "I couldn't live without him! He keeps being quarrelsome and it takes all my ingenuity to keep from making something out of it. And yet I have a feeling that he's unhappy and he'll snap out of it someday."

Betty looked thoughtful. "He does feel as if you're getting away from him," she said delicately. "He talked to me about it once."

Pat thrust out her lower lip, thinking about Betty's words. The signal came for the meeting and both girls sauntered down to the chapter room in silence.

Pat picked up a *Daily* lying on the floor near her and glanced over the calendar: tryouts for the next play, positions open for the student talent show staff (she had longed to be on that, but not now), political meetings, a senior speech recital on Thursday. The speech senior was Inga, one of her sorority sisters, and the chapter would go as a group. She'd love to hear Inga's program, but perhaps she ought to be studying with Tim that night. She weighed the choice and then she heard the chapter president gaveling for attention. The meeting began.

"Girls, I want you all to listen to this announcement," the president was saying. "Inga is giving her senior recital next Thursday, and the chapter will attend. We want to send her some red roses afterward."

Betty was going, of course, she told Pat as soon as chapter meeting ended.

"I don't think I can take the time," Pat said regretfully. "After those mid-term grades, I've simply got to study. Finals are only three weeks away."

"Oh, they'll excuse you all right," said Betty. "But you'll be missing a good program."

"I know."

She wondered if she was always going to have to choose like this, between Tim and all the things she wanted to do. She could have found time for the recital if she weren't so worried about being away from Tim that night. If he would only go to things like that with her! she thought in an anguish of frustration.

By the time Thursday night arrived she felt frustrated and irritable. She snapped at Dennis at the supper table, and he looked at her in amazement.

138

"What did I do now?"

"Oh, nothing," Pat said wearily. "I'm just so sick of everything."

Mrs. Marlowe looked at her daughter with concern.

"You're not trying to do too much, are you?"

"I'm not trying to do enough!" Pat snapped. "I'm just so sick of study, study, study — no fun, no activities, nothing else at all!"

Her father looked at her, about to reprove her for her ill-temper, and she said: "I'm sorry, Mother, I can't eat another thing. I've got a headache. I'm going up and lie down for an hour before I start studying."

Lying in her darkened room with a cold cloth on her head, because she really was getting a headache, she thought in a depressed mood that nothing seemed to be working out at all. She was worried almost sick about her final exams, the Alphas thought she was disloyal not to attend Inga's recital, the dean of the School of Speech thought she was showing too little interest in the speech department activities, she couldn't do any of the things she really wanted to do, she couldn't concentrate on her studies while she was so worried about Tim — and she could do nothing about him or any of her other problems, either. Doom seemed to be hanging over her like a black cloud, and there was nowhere to run, no way to escape it.

When Tim arrived she came downstairs slowly, still feeling almost ill. He looked at her with concern.

"What's the matter with you, honey?" he sounded so worried that she felt warm and reassured immediately. If she could just be seriously ill, that might be all she needed.

"I had a headache." She smiled at him wanly. "I've

been lying down. I think it's fretting over those finals that's got me down."

"You don't need to worry about the exams if you'd just settle down and work," he said. "I can help you. Where's that sample exam you had for geology?"

He began asking questions from the printed sheet and Pat gave the answers. Three or four she knew, many of them she had never heard of and had to look up and make notes about, some of them she guessed at, and invariably they were wrong.

"For Pete's sake!" Tim said in disgust, when they had finished the paper. "Don't you know any of your geology? No wonder you failed that mid-term! Didn't you ever learn how to work?"

"Certainly I learned how to work!" Pat snapped back, angry at his anger. "And what about your own econ grade? You don't need to talk to me about grades!"

"But at least I tried," Tim said. "You didn't even try. All right, now, go through again and see how many you remember out of the answers you looked up and made notes on."

At the end of the evening Pat knew quite a lot more geology than she had started with.

"I always seem to learn so much more when you are helping me," she said. "I appreciate this a lot, Tim. Do you want me to review you on your econ now?"

"No, thanks, I reviewed that with Betty this afternoon."

Chilled, she said only, "Well, will you help me again tomorrow night?"

"I'll see that you pass those exams," Tim said grimly, as if he had a moral obligation to fulfill.

They worked together for the next three weeks, drilling

140

for hours, and Pat felt confident that she could pass the final exams. She was also convinced, more than before, that she would not know how to study, what to do, where to turn, without Tim. She leaned on him, drawing comfort from the fact that he was there to lean on; she called him twice a day to ask his advice; she demanded his presence, and when he was out of sight she worried about him until she met him again.

However, she did pass the exams as Tim had promised her she would. And they celebrated the end of exam week and the vacation ahead of them on Saturday night with a bridge party with Betty and Joe.

Tim was gay, relaxed, and good-humored. Watching him play his cards with a small jest about each trick, Pat's own spirits rose. Everything had mended itself, just as she had believed it would. He was more like his old self tonight than he had been for weeks, and she thought, contentedly, that the past nightmare weeks had been due only to a mood. Next quarter would be different. . . .

"Let's go to church tomorrow," she said as she kissed Tim good night. "I'd like to go when I feel as good as I do now."

Besides, going to church meant she would see Tim at ten thirty in the morning. As she watched the lights of his car disappear, she was planning how she could have him stay for dinner, perhaps they could go for a ride all afternoon, of course they would be together in the evening. It was worth discarding all her plans and all her theater activities, if she attached Tim firmly again. Though subconsciously she knew that this jettisoning of all outside activity and interest was only temporary.

After church the next morning Tim was melancholy

again, and Pat, fear clutching at her heart, looked at his downcast mouth, his haggard eyes that looked sunken in gloom.

"Come on home and have dinner with us," she said as they got into the car. "Mother said she'd love to have you."

Tim looked at her, swallowed as if he were nerving himself up to a decision, and said, "Pat, I want to have a long talk with you."

All her anxieties swelled upon her like a tidal wave.

"You mean — about breaking up?"

"Yes."

He put the car into gear and concentrated on backing out of the parking space while Pat fumbled in her bag for a handkerchief. Tears were running down her cheeks, but she said nothing. As Tim eased into traffic and then turned into a quiet street she said, "When do you want to talk about it?"

"This afternoon. The sooner the better."

They were approaching the Marlowes, and Pat said hastily: "Let's go out by ourselves. I couldn't bear to face the family at a time like this. Will you go in and tell them we're going out for dinner?"

"Sure."

Tim parked the car, ran up the steps of the Marlowes' house, and disappeared. He reappeared in no time and said to Pat, "Your mother said that was fine."

Pat suppressed a nervous impulse to giggle hysterically. Little did her mother know what the purpose of this dinner was. She rode silently beside Tim while he searched for a spot where they would be unknown. Her thoughts ranged the past and the future like a camera picking up

142

two pictures at once. So much about this ride seemed so normal, so usual, so much like every ride with Tim, that it seemed impossible that they were looking for a place where they could "break up" permanently. As her mind repeated that phrase Pat shuddered and began to weep again. Tim stared at the road ahead, at parking spaces, at restaurant signs, as if he were unaware of her emotion. At last they found a place that looked almost empty, where they had never been before.

"We can be alone here," Tim said, parking the car.

They chose a booth, ordered coffee and hamburgers (Pat wondered why — she knew she wouldn't be able to swallow a mouthful), and sat back, staring at each other uncomfortably.

"But *why*, Tim?" Pat ventured, when the girl had taken their order, given them glasses of water, and gone away.

"Well," his eyes dropped from hers and he toyed with a menu nervously, "it's hard to explain, Pat. But I've been giving a lot of thought to this, all this past quarter. I'm confused and uncertain. All I know is that I don't want to marry you. And the way we're going, we'll drift into marriage and there we'll be. And what with the way we don't like to do anything together, what would it be like, after a year or so?"

"But, Tim, you don't know how I love you," Pat whispered. "You don't know what you're doing to me. I don't want anything, anything at all, except you."

He shook his head.

"But that wouldn't last," he said sadly. "You do want other things. You want the theater — you'd miss it too much if you gave it up for keeps."

143

"But I gave it up last quarter — after *A Doll's House*. Didn't you know?"

"Sure, I knew you weren't rehearsing any more. But if you couldn't ever go back to it, you'd miss it some-day —"

"But look how I'll miss you."

There was a silence.

"I'll miss you too." Tim's eyes filled with tears, and he blinked rapidly and blew his nose. "This isn't easy for me, either, Pat. But I think it will be best for you — maybe for both of us — if we break up now and see what happens."

She knew this was a final decision, and at the thought her head sank on her breast and she sobbed shamelessly and heavily. Once Tim would have taken her in his arms, one part of her mind kept reminding her; once he couldn't stand to see her tears, he would have petted and comforted her, and that was heaven. Now he sat stonily on the opposite side of the table, his eyes turned away from her, obviously suffering in his own way because of her suffering.

She tried to drink some of her coffee, she poked at her hamburger. But she was feeling almost ill, her heart was pounding so fast, and her stomach felt tied in knots. The waitress was watching them with active curiosity, but Pat didn't care. She leaned her elbows on the table and said plaintively: "But, Tim, couldn't we try again, some-way? We've been in love so long, how can we just stop like this? I'll love you till I die."

"I don't know how I can stand it," Tim said, entirely sincere. "But I've been thinking about it for a long time, and I've decided this is the only thing to do, and the only way to do it. We don't have much to talk about any more.

The only time we really have much fun is when we have Betty and Joe around."

"Is Betty to blame for this change?" Pat demanded bitterly.

He blushed red clear up to his eyes, but he looked at Pat steadily.

"I don't think it's Betty's fault," he said, and Pat winced at the confirmation of her suspicions. "It's just that, being in the math class together and working out problems together for that course, all of a sudden I realized what it's like to work with someone who likes the same things I like — like math and econ and so on. And you and I can't ever feel that way — "

He stopped and took a drink of water and tried to smile at Pat.

"Anyway, this doesn't have to be a permanent break," he suggested. "Just for the next three or four months we won't see each other — we'll go out with lots of other people, and see how it turns out."

"I don't want to go out with anyone else at all," Pat said unsteadily. At that moment she meant it. "I'll just wait till the time is over."

Tim was getting out of the booth and he held out his hand to help her past the table.

"Darling, I don't want to hurt you," he said, looking guilty and concerned again. "I think this will hurt less now than if we got married and then found we couldn't get along together."

"I know you're mistaken," Pat said, finding herself strangely calm now that the decision was taken, the doom she had dreaded had struck. "I'm as sure of it as I could possibly be. But you'll have to find out for yourself."

145

"I could be mistaken," Tim agreed. "This could be another growing-up mistake. But we've got to find out."

She was crying again. Waves of tearful despair seemed to alternate with moments of calm, and she wondered how she really felt. She thought, No more telephone calls, no more lunches together, no more rides to the campus in the mornings —

"Of course, I'll pick you up in the mornings as usual," Tim offered, as they stopped in front of her house.

"No, thanks!" Pat snapped. She was in one of her moments of calm, when she was mad rather than heartbroken. "I'll get myself down to school. Thanks just the same."

"Aren't you going to kiss me good-by?"

She slammed the car door violently.

"No, I'm not!"

She walked slowly up the sidewalk without looking back, head up, shoulders stiff, looking attentively at the fresh, feathery green misting the bushes along the walk, although she knew Tim sat there watching her until she went inside the house. She didn't care, she told herself. She was crying steadily again, and all she wanted was to lie on her bed alone with her heartbreak.

16

" Pat, for goodness' sake, whatever is the matter! "

Mrs. Marlowe met her daughter in the front hall as Pat started up the steps to her room, and her tone was comfortingly alarmed. Pat thought with a strange detachment: Isn't it funny? I haven't cried for ages, except for that little bit when I left the farm last summer, and now I can't seem to stop. She tried to respond to her mother's concern, and she found she could hardly talk.

" Tim's broken up with me! " she sobbed brokenly. " He's leaving me! I've lost him. Oh, Mother, I want to die."

Mrs. Marlowe steered her toward her room, supporting her up the stairs, talking as they went. "Pat, you'd better lie down for a while. You're worn out. This is a shock to me too. My goodness, I never expected Tim to be like this. Here, honey, get your dress off and lie down. I'll fix the shades — "

She drew the shades, threw a light blanket over Pat, brought her a pill with a glass of water. Pat turned on her radio, and the cheerful noise distracted her a little. Her long, shuddering sobs ceased, she felt calmer, and she said, lifting her head from the pillow: "I feel better, Mother. I think I'm not going to cry any more."

"If you can sleep it will be easier, Pat. The quicker the time passes, the better it will be."

"M-m-m-m-m." Pat was drowsy. "I think I can sleep for a while."

As she drifted off, her thoughts seemed orderly and composed, she faced the empty future calmly and indifferently. But when she woke a few hours later and opened her eyes on the void in her life, the thought of never talking to Tim again, never having him at her side, racked painfully through her mind, and she began to sob again.

However, a few hours had made some difference, even in the oblivion of sleep. When she had left Tim, in the first raw severance, she had wept for the past that was gone forever, for the first love that had changed into something unhappy and untenable, for memories that had become in a moment painful instead of delightful, for a foundation that had crumbled under her feet. Now already she was looking forward instead of back, and she wept in the nervous reaction to shock. While she sobbed, her mind was rising from its catastrophic blow and beginning to function. She thought: I can't go on like this. I've got to get over it.

She lay quiet a few more minutes. As soon as she told herself she must rise and exert herself, the quiescence of lying on her bed under a blanket, doing nothing, seemed to create a small world of comfort and safety that she was reluctant to leave. The sobbing passed away and again she felt calm. From somewhere a new strength she had never known before seemed to flow through her, and she got up and washed her face and prepared to face her family.

At the family supper table, her father looked sympathetic and at the same time determined to pull her willy-nilly through this stress.

"This is just one of those things," he said cheerfully. "Happens to everyone sometime. No use dwelling on it."

But at his words, to Pat's dismay, the tears flowed again. She sat at her place, inert, unable to eat, withdrawing inside of herself. Her emotions felt raw and tender, and when anyone tried to say anything they seemed to jump erratically away from any kind of comfort.

Mrs. Marlowe said: "If you don't want to eat, Pat, you don't have to. But try to drink some tea. It will make you feel better."

Obediently she drank some tea, and astonishingly it did make her feel better. She dried her eyes and concentrated on nothing.

Denny said, awed at the magnitude of her grief, "Isn't Tim going to come around any more at all?"

She shook her head, resolutely repressing the tears that threatened again at his name, and Mrs. Marlowe said: "Probably not, Denny. Don't discuss it."

"Why not?"

Something in Denny's astonishment touched a responsive chord. Pat smiled a dim smile and said, "That's just what I wonder." With some surprise, she noted that this effort at the light touch seemed actually to lighten the darkness.

She rose from the table and began to clear the dishes. Her father and brother departed for the Sunday evening TV shows. Her mother began washing the dishes in the kitchen, and Pat picked up a towel and dried them, finding comfort in her mother's presence, and an unsuspected need to cling to her at this time.

"I don't think I can sleep tonight," she said after a while. "I feel so shaken, Mother. I don't know what to do. I can't seem to stop thinking about it."

Her mother let her hands rest in the soapsuds a moment, as she drew her brows together in thought.

"If you could get away," she said, "that would help more than anything. The first three or four days are the hardest at a time like this, Pat. The main thing is to get through them as quickly as possible. How about going down to Mead and seeing Connie this week? She doesn't have her vacation for another fortnight."

To get away! To see Mead University, where she had thought of visiting sometime. To see Andy!

"Oh, Mother, that would be wonderful! I'd love to see Connie."

"Call her tonight and ask her if she could find a place for you to stay, and we'll see if we can send you off tomorrow."

Her erratic emotions jumped responsively at the idea of a complete change: Connie, whom she had not seen since Christmas; new boys — she reminded herself that she was free now, and must meet some new men as soon as possible; Andy — would he want to see her? He had thought Tim was wrong for her. He had said he wanted to know if she broke up. She wanted to see him and talk to him. But this she did not mention. Her mother's idea of seeing Connie was enough.

She called Mrs. Reid first for Connie's telephone number, and remarked casually that she might go down and visit her during this vacation week, pleased to hear her own voice sounding so normal, and then she rang the dormitory.

150

Connie was in the dorm; she reached the phone within a few minutes. Pat decided against revealing her sorrow by telephone. She was afraid she might break down again, and she knew that while Connie would urge her to come, even in tears, it would be better to tell her the story in person and, if possible, philosophically, as if she herself felt satisfied with the development. This would be impossible now, but already Pat found herself casting about for an approach that would be credible and ask for no sympathy.

"Pat?" Connie sounded astonished and pleased. "Hi, honey! How are you?"

"Mother says I can come down and visit you this week, if that's convenient for you," Pat said. "We've got vacation, and my exams are past."

"Lucky you! I've got to study all vacation for mine. I'd *love* to have you come. We'll be having classes, but you can go to some with me, and visit the campus in session. And there's a play scheduled for Thursday night. I think you'd like it."

It sounded delightful, and on that second level on which her mind seemed to be operating these days, Pat thought: Last week I couldn't have left Tim. Now I'm free; there's no reason why I can't do anything I want to. I'd love to go to a play again —

"Is there someplace I can stay?"

"You can stay in the dorm with me," Connie said promptly. "My roommate had to go home for ten days. Her mother is sick. This is a perfect time for you to come. Take that noon train from Chicago and I'll meet you at five o'clock."

"I'll be there." Pat was surprised at her own resilience. She had thought only two hours ago that she could never

151

be happy again. "Oh, and Connie —"

"Yes?"

"Will you call Andy and tell him I'm coming down? Tell him I want to see him too."

She hung up the telephone, restless again. She had suppressed the story of Tim's decision, and now she wanted to talk about it. She glanced at her watch. It was only seven.

"Mother, I think I'll go and see a sorority sister of mine. Julie Lombard — she lives in Evanston. May I take the car?"

"I think that's all right," her mother said. "But don't be out late. If you're taking a noon train tomorrow you've got to get some sleep, and you'll have to get up early to sort out your clothes and pack."

Julie would be home and glad to see her. Julie's own fiancé, Ted Stokely, had gone home to Iowa on vacation, and she was alone.

It was strange to be driving herself at night down to Evanston, Pat thought, when for months she had gone nowhere at night without Tim. Ah, well, this is something I'll have to get used to, she told herself, surprised, but pleased, that there were no more tears. She felt cut adrift, floating in a void, aimlessly, purposelessly. Somewhere out on a dark, hidden sea she knew some purpose was bobbing around like a buoy. How long before she could sight it? Something her mother had told her long ago, which she had paid no attention to at the time, came back to mind, and she dwelt on it, wondering why it had taken her so long to recognize the truth in it.

"When the apple is ripe, it will fall," her mother had said. "When you have grown enough to recognize some

152

facts of life, you will understand. It's a question of living long enough."

Her mother had said that last fall when she was talking about getting married, and Pat had ignored it. Now she turned the phrase over and over in her mind. When the time was right, Tim would come back. That thought was calming, and she clung to it. When the time was right, she would sight that hidden goal that she had glimpsed in high school and driven toward in college, for a short while. What had happened to it when her worry about Tim had blocked it? Why wasn't it there, now that he was gone? When the apple is ripe . . .

She parked in front of Julie's house and rang the bell.

"Hi, Julie. I wanted to talk to you. Tim and I broke up this afternoon."

"Oh, Pat, how terrible! I know just how you feel."

Julie's sympathy almost started the tears again, but Pat had come already to the point where she felt they were wasting time, and resolutely she kept them back and forced herself to calmness. Julie led her to the back of the house where they could be alone in the sunroom, and sat down beside her.

"I thought maybe you could give me some advice," Pat said. "I knew you had broken up with Ted last summer."

"Oh, it was hideous," Julie assured her. "I thought I'd die. I couldn't stop crying for two days, and Mother was worried sick. But then I went back to work and made up my mind that I'd forget him, and I dated everyone I could find. I must have gone out with a dozen boys."

This seemed to Pat like an inordinate effort, for which she was just too tired.

"What do you think was the reason?" she asked.

153

"We were together too much." Julie's eyes shadowed as if remembering that part of it was still painful. "We quarreled quite a lot, and there wasn't enough to do. And I know I was too demanding. I made him come over every night, even when he wanted to study at home. I made him go everywhere with me. And I talked about getting married all the time. That's a mistake that's so easy to make! We had planned to get married, and I thought the more I talked about it the more definite it would be, and instead it made him back off."

"That's just what happened with Tim and me," Pat marveled. "I can see how it was my fault." Acknowledging her own errors made her feel stronger. "But how did you get him back again?"

"He came back after about three months." Julie smiled. "He'd gone out with half a dozen girls and found he missed me after all. And when he came back I was very casual. I acted as if we were just getting acquainted, I took nothing for granted, I never asked him for a favor or to come over. I made him do all the chasing, and let him feel as if I weren't quite sure now whether I was interested or not. And then when he talked about marriage —"

"You set a date," Pat said, knowing that part of the story.

"We're getting married in August," Julie said, looking at her ring.

"We were going to get married in August," Pat said, wincing. To sidetrack the tears that threatened, she said quickly: "I feel so helpless. What can I do?"

"Nothing," Julie said firmly. "Ignore him. If he broke up because you were too possessive, you'll have to leave him very strictly alone. Don't write, don't telephone, don't even ask the girls about him. Don't let him think you care."

She leaned forward comfortingly.

"He'll come back," she said. " After two and a half years of being in love, it couldn't break up so completely. This is only a phase. You know they always say everyone breaks up at least once before they know it's for sure. But in the meantime, go out with everyone who asks you. You have to get to the point where you don't care whether he does or not, before you're safe. And make yourself a different girl before he does."

17

MR. AND MRS. MARLOWE took Pat to the train the next day. The fact that her father took the day out of his office signified how deeply he felt her need, how important he considered this step. Pat herself, after touching heights of confidence last night when she had talked to Julie, was low again, unable to eat, finding every step in getting ready an effort that exhausted her. Once she said to her mother: "Going to Mead isn't going to help that much, Mother. I can't get over Tim."

"No, of course not, after all this time," her mother agreed with her. "But it's easier to get adjusted to a blow like this in a new place with new people around you. By next Friday when you come home, things will be easier."

Pat looked dubious. "I feel as if I ought to let Tim know I'm going to be out of town."

"No," said Mrs. Marlowe sharply. "Whatever you do, Pat, don't telephone him. And *don't write*."

"I'm not going to write," Pat said, weary and docile.

"But be *sure* you don't." Her mother sounded as if she feared Pat's resolution might collapse when she was once away from home. She was folding slips and tucking nylon hose into a divided plastic bag for traveling. "Honey, this is absolutely fundamental. One line and he is likely to think you're still trying to keep in touch with him. If he wants to break off, let it be his decision when to get in touch again. Furthermore, if he hears nothing from you for days or weeks he can't help but be a little curious. He's going to wonder how you're getting along without him, what you're doing with yourself. Let him wonder! It'll do more good than telling him. When he gets curious enough, he'll call you to find out."

Pat heard her mother in silence. She had planned to write to Tim the moment she got on the train, convinced that when he heard she had gone out of town for a week he would miss her and answer the letter, possibly even drive down to Mead while she was there. Her daydream had gone so far as to visualize him hunting anxiously for her on the campus, and taking her in his arms to assure her that he had been out of his mind with alarm when he had realized, the day after she left, what he had done. This was a delightful dream, and it was not easy to discard it.

" Pat," her mother said again.

" Yes, Mother."

" If you ever want your life to come out the way you hope " — she did not mention Tim, Pat noted — " you must believe what I'm telling you."

Pat discarded the dream then, but the effort left her melancholy and fatigued again. She nibbled futilely at a piece of toast and managed to drink a cup of tea. In silence she rode down to Chicago, wondering why she was going away and then why she should ever come back.

Listlessly she climbed upon the train, kissed her parents farewell, and opened a magazine to a crossword puzzle.

157

Right now she was numb, and that was a more comfortable state than the earlier condition, where acute pain seemed to shoot through her thoughts, succeeded by horrifying sensations of total emptines. She hoped the numbness would last until she got to Mead, when she might be able to deaden her emotions with people, activity, noise, laughter, excitement. If only she didn't have to think! Because her thoughts were intolerable.

An hour later she went to the dining car, not because she thought she could eat anything, but because it was something to do. An engaging young soldier on leave sat across from her, and almost without thinking, in an automatic reaction, Pat smiled at him. By the time her ham sandwich was served they were talking cheerfully. She asked him about his home town, and he told her about his family and the girl who had written him a "Dear John" letter only a month ago. He seemed to have accepted the girl's defection very calmly, Pat thought, feeling that they had a great deal in common. She told him she had broken up with her boy friend too, and was going to visit a friend at Mead to get over it, and he seemed interested and sympathetic.

It was one of those passing exchanges that reaffirm one's confidence in human relations, and when Pat returned to her car she felt as if a great deal of time had passed, as if already she was in a new stage of her life, stronger, able to look back without wild regret, ready to look forward. Now she was eagerly anticipating the week at Mead, she could hardly wait to see Andy, she could even smile a little at the shock and horror Connie would feel at her news. She felt much brighter, and not only surprised, but even amused at herself, for a state of mind that only yesterday she had believed she could never achieve again.

And then she wondered if she was fickle and unstable to have allowed herself to feel cheerful so soon. This breakup was like a death in the family, and it seemed as if, out of respect to her lost love, she should continue mourning a little longer than twenty-four hours.

Was it only this time yesterday that she had come home from her last talk with Tim, shattered and inconsolable? The thought made her heart race again, her stomach tighten in anguish, her mind coast into black depths for a moment, and she contemplated her reactions with some satisfaction. She had meant what she said to Tim and to her mother yesterday, when she had said she'd love him until she died, and she was not ready yet to give up that dedicated future.

The train arrived at Greeneville, Indiana, pulling into the station and slowing down. Pat stood at the top of the steps, her bag beside her, watching the platform slide by until the train stopped. She saw a dozen interesting-looking students, mostly boys, watching the train, and she remembered that part of her purpose in coming to Mead was to meet some new men. She stepped onto the platform, and Connie came racing down from the far end.

"Oh, Pat, I'm so glad to see you!" Connie threw her arms around her and kissed her enthusiastically. "You look wonderful."

She shouldn't, Pat's mind noted. She should be looking drawn and haggard. But she smiled brightly and said: "I'm so glad to be here. Did you tell Andy I was coming?"

"He said he'd call you at the dorm tonight after supper," Connie reported. She picked up Pat's bag and turned toward the exit. "We're only about six blocks from the dorm, so we'll walk. Lucky it's a nice day."

The little Indiana town was south of Chicago and two weeks ahead in spring bloom. They passed gardens brilliant with daffodils, old white houses framed in forsythia, early tulips, green lawns.

"Everything is so pretty," Pat said appreciatively. "Nothing was in bloom at home yet."

"Oh, spring is the loveliest season down here. Look at that patch of blue scilla! We have violets blooming at the Zeta house. I'm sorry you missed the crocuses. But it's so wonderful to have you visiting. How did you happen to decide to come just at this time?"

"Well —" Pat debated how to tell Connie, and decided to make the news as dramatic as it deserved to be. "Tim and I have broken up."

"No!" Connie stopped short and set the suitcase down on the sidewalk. "Why, Pat! I never thought — I mean, you and Tim always — Why, just last Christmas everything was — What on earth happened?"

"I'll carry that bag — it's heavy." Pat picked up the bag and they went on, walking more slowly. "It was very sudden, and I'm not used to it yet. Anyway, I was very shaken, naturally."

"Naturally."

"Mother gave me a pill to calm my nerves." In retrospect this medication seemed to emphasize the dire effects of the crisis. "She was worried because I couldn't eat, couldn't sleep. And then she thought I ought to get away for a few days, and I remembered that you wanted me to visit you down here, and this seemed like a good time."

Overhead the sky was blue and the trees were misty

160

with the fresh green of unfurling buds. The sun, low in the sky, shot golden rays across their path, and the new green of the spring grass looked like velvet where the sun struck. A bed of pink and blue and white hyacinths scented the air with fresh and stirring fragrance, and Pat drew a deep breath. Suddenly she was tired of talking about the past twenty-four hours. She wanted to forget. She wanted to enjoy herself.

"We'd been together too much," she said rapidly and casually. "And I think he was getting tired. Anyway, it's all over, and I want to have fun while I'm here."

Connie looked at her with respect for her strength in putting tragedy behind her, and said: "You'll have a wonderful time. You'll love the girls at the Zeta house. The Alphas are nice too. I called a friend of mine at their house, and they want you to have lunch with them tomorrow. And another girl I know, in speech here, wants to take you to class with her. And of course Andy is calling tonight. I think you'll have plenty to do."

They arrived at the Zeta house and Connie took her up to her room, where the windows opened on the setting sun behind a maple tree just unfolding tiny red leaves. She met forty Zetas at dinnertime, all of them friendly, gay, sparkling, and talking about persons and events on the Mead campus that reminded Pat of home, yet were fascinatingly different. The food was delicious, and for the first time since church yesterday Pat found she could enjoy it.

At seven o'clock a call came for her, and Andy said: "Hi, Pat! What gives? When I heard you were on our campus I wanted to say hello."

"Andy, I'm so glad to be here," Pat said, feeling at the

sound of his voice almost like her old self. "I haven't seen a play since Christmas. I haven't had a chance to talk theater since you were home."

"How come you're visiting?"

"I broke up with Tim yesterday, and I had to get away from it all for a few days."

"Well, congratulations! This I've been waiting to hear. Is it for real?"

"Oh, yes," she said, sounding more assured than she wanted to, and wondering how else to say it. "At least, we aren't going to see each other again for months, and I'm forgetting the whole thing and getting used to having fun without any strings."

"I'll be around to see you at eight o'clock," he said promptly. "I've got a mid-semester tomorrow, so I'll have to leave to study by ten o'clock. But we can go out and have a Coke somewhere."

"Fine. Connie has a chapter meeting anyway, so she can't be with me this evening."

"I'll make it seven thirty."

They walked down to "the Greek's," where Andy told her the whole campus congregated for coffee and Cokes, and over coffee they talked again the way they had always talked when they got together.

"I'll take you to a rehearsal tomorrow at two," Andy said, when he took her back to the Zeta house five minutes before the deadline. "You'll love this. It's an experimental thing that seems weird until you get into it, but the director here has all sorts of ingenious ideas for business and interpretation that are very challenging. I don't know how the audience is going to take it, but for the cast it's fascinating."

162

"Oh, Andy, I hadn't realized how much I'd missed the theater since last January," Pat told him. "I tried to shut it out when I realized it was coming between Tim and me, and I stayed away from play rehearsals. I even stopped reading about plays and thinking about them, and I think it did something to me. Tonight makes me feel so good. I *love* it."

The days passed too quickly, filled with everything Pat loved: play rehearsals (the director, at Andy's suggestion, put Pat into a crowd scene so she could be part of the play), attractive boys who were flatteringly attentive to a feminine visitor, the Alphas who were almost as nice as her own chapter, Andy taking her out for rehearsals and coffee afterward every night. Connie took her to classes, ate dinner with her every evening, and they talked after lights were out every night.

Thursday and Friday nights the play was being performed, and Saturday Pat would return home. The play went very well, although the audience seemed confused, as Andy had predicted they would be. But Pat and Andy, with the rest of the cast, held a celebration party following the last performance, and laughed over the obscure points they all felt sure the audience had missed.

Pat felt as if she were a new person in a different world from the one she had left only last Monday. She fell silent toward the end of the evening, contemplating this change in her life, wishing she could stay on here, and knowing that this very weekend she must return to Allandale and pick up the pieces of the life she had left there. She could consider that life with detachment here at Mead. She wondered exactly how it would hit her when she was back at Northwestern.

163

"Penny for your thoughts," Andy said, sliding a coin across the table to her. The other students had left them to join a party outside of town, and she was glad to be alone with Andy.

"I'm thinking about going home tomorrow," she said sadly. "I wish I didn't have to. I've loved it down here, and I've had such fun with you."

He reached across the table for her hand and his eyes gleamed sardonically.

"Fun you never had with Tim, I'll bet."

"How true. I missed an awful lot."

"I kept telling you, and you didn't believe me."

"I knew I was missing something, but I didn't know how much. I still don't know exactly. I mean, when I think of Tim, I get all mixed up. If he came back next week, I don't know what I'd do — "

Andy withdrew his hand, but his eyes were understanding.

"It'll take you awhile to get straightened out. I can wait; I'm not in a hurry. I want to see you week after next when I come home for vacation, and we'll just have fun."

She knew what he meant, and she was grateful. He wasn't telling her he loved her. He didn't want her on a rebound, he didn't want her to make a mistake a second time. Already, her mind noted, she was thinking of Tim as "a mistake." Was he? Or was the breakup a mistake?

She still could not be sure of either answer.

18

ANDY SAW HER OFF for Chicago the next day with Connie.

"I'll be home in one more week," he said, as he handed her up the steps. "I'll see you then, and we'll do the town."

"It's been a wonderful, wonderful week," she told both of them. "I can't thank you enough. I feel like a different person."

She settled back, smiling and waving through the window until the train pulled out, and then she began, thoughtful and contented, to consider the person she was, the person she must become, the future she must face.

Alone, with no one to give her moral support after the week of company and companionship and hectic activity, she deliberately turned her thoughts to Tim, testing her own strength. She could think of him calmly, she found, probing with a thought like a needle here and there. She could accept the fact that they had been together too much, had worn out their love by expecting it to do too much for them, without enough underpinning to support it. So it had given way beneath her and plunged her life into chaos. She considered that concept, rather pleased with it, and approached the thought more closely: in another few hours she would be in Chicago, back where she had started less than a week ago.

Without warning, her mind took off on an uncontrollable, vaulting daydream: Suppose Tim met the train? Suppose she saw him there, just as he would have been any other time that she had gone out of town? He would take her in his arms and tell her —

Panicky, she realized where her thoughts were leading her; she was getting upset again, she was going to cry. She tried to think about Andy and Mead and those nice boys in the play who had been so attentive. Tim's image kept intruding.

Good heavens, she thought, I can't go back home right where I was when I left. I've got to stop thinking about him.

It was disconcerting to discover that the cure had been so short-lived. She had felt so happy at Mead, she had thought she had found quick comfort, the sweet sedative that would let her grow accustomed to a new life without effort or pain. She opened her eyes and sat upright, disillusioned. So it was not going to be easy after all. She felt defrauded, as if someone had promised her something and then failed to deliver.

But there was a certain satisfaction in heartbreak. Painful as it was, it lent her some distinction — it made her newsworthy. She began thinking about the way she would tell everyone when she returned to school on Monday. The girls at the Alpha house would be astonished. This breakup would be the subject of the day at the Grill.

She paused. Could she go to the Grill daily, if Tim was there — with Betty?

She went from that question to another. How could she fill all those empty hours of time that she had spent with

166

Tim? The coming days seemed suddenly so confused, the answers so mixed and unsatisfactory, that she was fatigued with her thoughts and bored with being alone. She went through the train to the club car and found a couple of students also returning from vacations in Indiana, and spent the rest of the trip playing cards and exchanging campus experiences.

The train pulled into the station at Chicago, and Pat, deadening her thoughts with conversation, picked up her bag, bade farewell to the new friends of the train trip, and started down the platform to meet her parents at the gate. Hammering in her mind was the question, Will Tim be there?

Of course he won't, she told herself, trying to be impatient with such foolishness. But hope kept insisting: Perhaps he changed his mind, perhaps he is frantic about the way he acted. Her heart was pounding so her breath came fast, and she quickened her steps, walking as fast as her high-heeled shoes and heavy bag would permit.

Her parents were waiting at the gate, and her eager gaze ranged beyond them, looking, looking, searching, hoping. Hope died easily, with hardly a flicker of surprise. Tim was not there.

But of course, she told herself, kissing her mother and crying aloud: "I had a wonderful time, Mother. Mead is a lovely place — everyone was so nice to me. I loved it."

Her mother was looking at her closely, she noted, as she turned to her father and kissed him. What change did she expect to find?

The excitement and suspense of home-coming died away, leaving ashes of letdown and fatigue. Pat felt suddenly as if she could hardly drag her bag another step.

Gratefully she handed it to her father and followed her parents across the wide marble floor, up long, curving steps to the door, and down the street a block and a half to the car. She sank down in the back seat, exhausted and silent, as her father turned the car toward Allandale.

She was almost home again; she was back where everything reminded her of Tim — every landmark on the Outer Drive she had observed on some ride with him — the lake, gleaming quiet under the late afterglow of a rosy sky, the gulls, rising and swooping about the piles.

She winced and closed her eyes. The battle was still ahead of her, and all the dreams she had dreamed, all the gay conversations she had planned, all the shock and surprise and astonishment she would create were nothing. Nothing at all.

"I'm glad you had a good time," her mother remarked from the front seat. " What did you do? "

" Did I tell you I saw Andy? He took me to play rehearsal and got me into a crowd scene." As she described that experience, she began to remember more clearly, and the week just past became alive again.

" That's wonderful," her mother said. " You know, honey, it seemed to me before — well, before spring vacation, you were getting very monotonous, kind of drab and uninteresting and colorless. I was very depressed about it. And now you're alive again. You're sparkling the way you used to."

Pat said nothing, but she thought about her mother's words. So she had become drab. Tim had made her that way, and yet that might have been why she lost him in the end. She lifted her chin, suddenly angry as if she had been beaten in an unfair fight.

168

"I'm going back into the plays this quarter," she said aloud. "Everything I can get into. I never realized how much I was missing."

"I knew you were cutting out a lot of things that made you an interesting person," her mother said. "You depended too much on someone else. Never let yourself need anyone again the way you thought you needed Tim, Pat. It kills your personality."

Pat knew what she meant. The process of release had been painful, and still, after this past week, a sudden memory, a familiar fragrance, a remembered melody, would jab her heart with sudden despair. But she could cope with it more quickly from now on. Within a short time she knew, not daydreaming but knowing from experience, she would be able to ignore these jabs of pain until they ceased to attack her.

When she got into the house she was prepared for an emotional struggle, and somewhat to her surprise, nothing happened. Evidently in so short a time as a week the pain had become erratic. She had an impulse born of two years' habit to ask if anyone had called — had there been any mail? Resolutely she kept it down and went upstairs with her bag.

All Tim's pictures were gone! A rush of anger swept over her, and then subsided. She had expected to look at all her pictures again and weep over the past. Perhaps it was better this way.

"Mother?" she called. "What have you done with my pictures?"

"I put them away," her mother answered calmly. "They're in a box in the attic. Any time you want them you can have them. I thought perhaps you wouldn't want them when you got home."

"Well —"

Here it was Saturday evening, a night Tim had always been with her. The first of the empty hours to fill. She emptied her bag hastily, tossing clothes into the laundry, hanging up dresses, thinking as she worked.

Spring tryouts would be held next week. She found her university calendar and looked up dates. There was an important spring dance two weeks from last night. She'd get one of the Alphas to find her a date. Or perhaps Andy would still be in town on his vacation. It could be really fun to go to a dance with a new boy, just for a change.

She could feel herself shedding a chrysalis that had been chokingly tight because she had stayed within it too long. She felt as if something had snapped and left her free, as she had not been free for two and a half long years. And she had been afraid of freedom, so unused to it was she.

She still found it difficult to believe what her mother had meant when she said Pat had lost her sparkle. All she knew now, in these first hours of home-coming, was that she felt as if she had grown up in this past week.

She could think of so many things she wanted to do in school that she had passed by in the last two quarters. Anything could happen, and she was free to choose, to play, to do almost anything she wanted.

Her mother came in to say that supper was ready.

"I've been thinking about Andy," she remarked. "He sounds kind of hasty to me. You're not going to get mixed up in another romance in too much of a hurry, are you?"

Pat laughed aloud.

"I'm not going to fall in love again for a long, long

170

time," she said, knowing that she meant it. " It takes too much time, there are too many other things to do first."

Her mother looked relieved, but unconvinced. Pat looked at her thoughtfully, and she spoke slowly, thinking about her words as she said them.

" I don't know if I'd take Tim back now, if he did come. If he did, I'd understand him better, and perhaps he wouldn't be the same. But there's no hurry about anything. I've got three more years of college after this one, and there is so much to do with them! "

When she met love again, with Tim or with someone else, she knew, without saying it yet, it would be a new kind of love: a love that would let her flower, instead of distorting her personality as her first love had done. When she met love again it would give her something instead of taking it away. But not too soon, she thought, as she followed her mother downstairs.

Not too soon.

Biography of Anne Emery

ANNE EMERY was born Anne Eleanor McGuigan in Fargo, North Dakota. She has lived in Evanston, Illinois, since she was nine years old, and there she attended Evanston Township High School and took a B.A. degree at Northwestern University.

Following her graduation, her father, a professor of pharmacology and therapeutics at the University of Illinois, took the family abroad for a year, where they visited his birthplace in Northern Ireland and toured the British Isles, France, Switzerland, and Italy. She spent nine months studying at the University of Grenoble in France.

Upon return, Anne McGuigan taught in the Evanston schools — four years in the seventh and eighth grades at Haven Intermediate School, and, after her marriage in 1933 to John D. Emery, six more years in the fourth and fifth grades at Orrington School.

Then she retired from teaching to keep house and take care of her family. There are five young Emerys: Mary, Kate, Joan, Robert, and Martha. Mary and Kate are in college this year, Joan and Robert are in high school, and Martha is in seventh grade.